Nicholas Fisk has had a number of different occupations. He's served in the RAF, and been an actor in an Irish Shakespeare company, a book editor, a jazz musician, a journalist, worked in advertising and as a freelance publishing consultant. He's now a highly successful author with well over forty books to his credit, as well as several television scripts.

He is particularly well known for his science fiction titles, such as *Grinny, A Rag, A Bone and A Hank of Hair, Time Trap* and, of course, *Backlash*. For Walker Books, he has also written *The Worm Charmers*, a thriller for children, and *The Model Village*, a picture book.

Nicholas Fisk is married with four children and lives in Hertfordshire.

"A most original writer ... the Huxley-Wyndham-Golding of children's literature." *Joy Whitby, Twentieth Century Children's Writers*

Also by Nicholas Fisk

BACKLASH

NICHOLAS FISK

WALKER BOOKS
LONDON

First published 1988 by Walker Books Ltd
87 Vauxhall Walk, London SE11 5HJ

This edition published 1991

Printed and bound in Great Britain by
Cox &Wyman Ltd, Reading, Berkshire

British Library Cataloguing in Publication Data
Fisk, Nicholas
Backlash.
I. Title
823'.914 [F]
ISBN 0-7445-1331-6

CONTENTS

The Capture

"I can't, I can't," Boo moaned, and let himself fall on his face on the strange, rubbery, purplish undergrowth. He buried his head in his arms. His legs thrashed feebly. His body heaved. Tears spilled over his plump arms.

"If he can't, he can't," Leo said, "and that's all there is to it. He's only four."

Behind them, they could hear the sounds of the Doops. The Doops were chasing them, hunting them down. Very soon, the Doops would catch them.

"Could we carry him?" Mina said, gasping the words.

"*Carry* him!" Leo answered. "You're joking! I can hardly stagger!"

Leo was nearly eleven. His sister Mina was twelve. They were tall, strong and well made: typical Earthside children of their time, the middle of the twenty-first century. But they were exhausted. Almost done for.

"They're getting closer," Mina said. Her head was cocked like a frightened animal's. She could hear the Doops – their whooping cries, the rattle of their weapons, the harsh commands of their leader – but she could not see them. The "trees" and "plants" hid them. She shuddered.

Everything about Argosy IV was alien and horrible. The "trees" were great slippery tubes, flesh-coloured and glistening, topped with leaves like ragged spears. The "plants" were either the rubbery, purple things on which little Boo lay sobbing, or writhing tangles of what could have been animal entrails, fleshy, wet, sodden, stinking. The *Galaxy Manual* said: "Argosy IV, though a planet of some interest to the botanist, offers few other attractions to the Earthside visitor." Mina had read the words on the journey to Argosy. They rang true.

"We've *got* to get on, we *must* do something," she said. "Boo, listen to me! Get up, Boo!"

"Won't," Boo said. "Can't." He kicked his stained legs.

"You can. You must."

Far above their heads, there was a fleshy *splat*! Then another. "More nets," Leo hissed. "Come on, *move*!"

They pulled Boo to his feet and dragged him, blubbering, through the undergrowth. Above them, the Doops' bullets smacked into the trees and released the nets. The nets fell almost like sheets of rain. You had to run like mad to escape their fine, immensely strong meshes. Boo could not run fast enough. Leo said, "Mina – grab an arm and a leg each, OK?" Before, they had tugged Boo along by his arms. Now he was spreadeagled, flying above the undergrowth. It was a good idea: they got on

10

faster. Behind them, the nets lazily showered down, catching nothing. Leo and Mina groaned, sweated and stumbled on, deeper into the forest.

But always, the Doops came closer.

They reached a different place, a sort of clearing, with sullen grey rocks jutting out from the ground, and dead and dying trees that could not live with the rocks. Mina gasped, "Rest!"

They collapsed, panting; then looked for hiding places in the rocks. There were some small caves and caverns, but what good would they be? The Doops would smell them out one way or another.

"I'm going to take a look," Leo said, nodding his head at a dead, dried-out tree. Its trunk had fallen at an angle to the ground. He crawled up and along it on all fours. Sometimes the scabby bark gave way and his foot slipped on the soapy trunk beneath. Leo tottered, swore and clung on for dear life.

But when he reached the crown of the tree, he was rewarded. The advancing Doops could not see him: the tree's sword-like leaves hid him. But he could see the Doops.

There were perhaps thirty of them, fanned out. Their bodies and heads looked human. This did not surprise Leo. Doops were called Doops because they had been designed as duplicates – human-like, artificial beings imitating men and women. Their structures even included human elements: cloned flesh and bone, laboratory-produced kits of human genes and structures. The rest was electronics and engineering, computers and gadgetry.

"Doop-a-doop-a-doop, leave it to your Doop!" the old ads had promised.

11

Mow the lawn?
Mind the kids?
Paint the shed?
Serve the soup?
Now you've got it easy! Now you've got a Doop!

Leo had heard a lot about Doops. Now he saw them.
What he saw frightened him.

They were good. Much too good. They moved too
easily, too humanly. They were too well muscled, too
alert-looking. In the TV ads, they were always shown
as mild-mannered servants; these Doops looked anything but mild.

Two things surprised him. First, he thought that
every Doop would exactly resemble every other Doop.
It wasn't so. There were considerable differences, apart
from the obvious difference of male and female. Some
Doops were tall, some stocky, some dark, some fair.
The human designers of the Doops must have been
brilliant genetic engineers.

The second surprise was the Doops' dress – gaudy,
noisy, outrageous. They had adorned themselves with
metal or plastic jewellery, with curving swords, with
glittering helmets and thonged sandals. They bellowed,
screeched, pranced and flourished their weapons.

The leader was the most outrageous of them all.
Her black hair flowed and waved like a dark sea over
her golden skin. With her right hand, she brandished
a spear; in her left, she held a jewel-crusted globe.
Amplifier inside it, Leo thought. That's why her
screechings sound so loud.

Below him, Mina called, "What can you see? What's
happening?" Boo's face looked up at him too. "I'm
hungry," he said. He sounded like a juvenile foghorn.

"I've got to *eat*!"

Leo shouted down to them. "There's a lot of them, and they've got a leader. She's — "

"She?" Mina called back. "Did you say, 'she'?"

"Yes, a woman. Well, a female, anyhow."

"What are they doing?"

"They're still coming on, they're all dressed up like warriors — "

"*I'm hungry.*"

"Shut, up, Boo. Listen, Mina, we'll have to stay here, there's nothing around us but more jungle. We'll have to surrender!"

"Oh no we won't! I'm not giving myself up! Or Boo!"

"*Hungry.* Oh, boo. Oh, boo-hoo. Boo-hoo-*hoo*!"

Leo thought, Boo always starts crying the same way, first of all a "boo", then the rest of it. Out loud, Leo said, "Shut *up*, Boo." He stared at the Doops. He was chilled with fear. They were getting closer and closer.

Mina said, "I'm coming up! Boo, stay there and don't move and stop crying or I'll skin you alive."

She began clambering along the sloping, treacherous tree trunk. Boo watched her with big eyes still wet with tears. His mouth pouted but he did not cry. Leo thought, You're a good little man. Well, you *have* to be good if your parents zoom you round all the nastiest bits of the Galaxy in crummy ships that keep going wrong...

"Good boy, Boo, you're a good boy!" he shouted.

Boo said, "Good," then "Hungry!"

Mina was beside Leo now. They silently watched the Doops. "They know where we are, don't they?" Mina whispered. "I suppose they've got all sorts of sensors and sonars and thermotrackers..."

"Course they know," Leo said. "So there's no need to whisper. They're coming for us. They'll get us."

"That woman," Mina said in an awed voice. "She's *awful*! If she gets us – if she gets hold of Boo..."

"She won't do anything," Leo said. "I mean, the Doops are *programed*, they wouldn't actually *harm* us..." His words tailed off.

Now the leader-woman was carried on the shoulders of two tall warrior Doops. She was jerking her spear above her head, thrusting it towards Leo and Mina and Boo. Her yelling mouth was a black hole fringed with very white teeth and red lips. Leo could see every detail. The Doops were that close.

"I'm going to run," Mina said. She started shuffling backwards down the trunk. "I won't let them catch me, I won't let them hurt Boo."

Leo did not hear her. Something extraordinary was happening. A prancing, shouting Doop warrior had been dancing about on the edge of a rocky ledge. He fell. Leo saw the rock give way, and the Doop's legs flailing, and his body fall and fall, in an ugly, jarring series of thumps and batterings; and then the body just lay there, almost hidden by the purple undergrowth. It lay motionless.

Immediately, the Doops' war cries were silenced. They forgot the chase and gathered round the fallen body. The woman leader bent over the body. She examined it for a long time. Then she stood erect, threw back her head, tore at her long black hair and howled.

"Mina!" Leo called, "Come back! Come and see!"

She crawled up to him. Both watched as the Doops threw down their weapons and gathered round their leader and the body in the undergrowth. They began to howl like wolves, like banshees, like lost spirits. The greenish sky of Argosy IV seemed to quiver at the noise. The planet's thick, dank air vibrated with it. Mina and Leo looked and listened and were appalled.

But then, after many minutes, Mina said, "But why — but why are they making so much *fuss*? I mean, they're warriors, and warriors get killed... You'd think it was the end of the world for them!"

"It's one step nearer," Leo said.

"What do you mean?"

"Well, look: there are only so many Doops in the whole Universe, right? Because we stopped making them when they turned out to be a mistake. And they can't breed, can't reproduce themselves. When this lot dies, the whole race dies. Extinct. No more Doops. So every death is a disaster. So they make a big fuss."

Beneath them Boo foghorned. "I want to *tell* you something."

"What?"

"I'm *hungry*."

For the first time on Argosy IV, Mina and Leo laughed.

"Back to normality," Mina said, rolling her eyes.

"If you call this normality," Leo said. He began his descent of the tree. "I mean, first we're castaways and soon we'll be captives. And Boo's hungry..."

Mina began her descent. "Well, at least the Doops have lost interest in us. We're not going to be boiled in a pot, or anything."

"Skin you alive," Boo suggested from the ground.

Mina grinned at Boo with deliberate cheerfulness. She was used to being brave, used to dangers and dramas. But Boo must not know how bad things were.

A piece of bark skidded away under her foot. She clung to the trunk and, taking her time, looked about

15

for a safe foothold. Looking, she glimpsed the Doops in the distance. "Leo!" she said, in a sort of gasp. "Leo, come back! Look!"

Suddenly, the Doops had lost interest in mourning the dead body. Suddenly their weapons were picked up – their leader was once again perched triumphantly on the shoulders of two warriors – the Doops were waving weapons, shouting their war cries and heading, menacingly, for Mina, Leo and Boo.

The chase was on again.

The sudden switch of mood and actions panicked Leo and Mina. They half fell and half scrambled from their tree, snatched Boo, and ran into the jungle-like forest.

The undergrowth became thicker, the trees closer. Again Boo was carried spreadeagled. "My arms are pulling out!" he cried.

Behind them the cries of the Doops sounded closer. Above them, the occasional net-bullet thumped dully into a tree and the net cascaded down like lazy rain-water. But the forest was too thick, the nets snagged in the trees.

Leo's accident halted them. He said, "Ouch!" stumbled – fell – and his face went white. "Hole in the ground," he said. "Ankle... hurting..." Then he began swearing. Boo listened delightedly to the swear words and from time to time said, "I heard that!" But then he noticed how white and twisted Leo's face was, and looked solemn.

"It's no good, Mina, I can't go on," Leo said quietly. As he spoke, a net blossomed from a tree above them and floated down, glistening. "That's it, then," Leo said. He lay back and watched the net come. It touched his face and hands like cold spiders' webs. Mina held

Boo close. The net covered them. She said, "They won't really *do* anything, will they, Leo? You said so yourself – they're *programed* not to..."

The net covered all three of them. Leo tested the strands with clawed fingers, trying to wrench them apart. Useless. They were as fine and strong as carbon-fibre filaments.

Suddenly a Doop warrior was in front of them, grinning and prancing and waving his curved sword in their faces. Then three more of them. Mina and Leo kept their faces expressionless and their mouths closed. Boo, in his foghorn voice, said, "Show-off." He was not crying. He had sensed that the situation was too serious to cry about.

The Warrior Queen was among the last to come. She slid easily from the shoulders of the men carrying her. Mina and Leo stared at her. Close to, she seemed beautiful and wild and dark; stupid – some of her jewelled ornaments cut into her flesh, and there was too much of everything; and above all, frightening. Her human-looking eyes had no humanity in them. They were as cold as the eyes of a cat.

The first warrior with the curved sword said, "I was first. I kill them. OK?" He cut at the air with his sword and showed his teeth. The Warrior Queen shrugged. The sword was raised.

Before it could fall, the jewelled globe in the Warrior Queen's hand spoke. "I want them," it said. "Bring them to me." It was the voice of a young girl.

"OK," said the Warrior Queen, emotionlessly.

Her bearers lifted her to their shoulders. She spoke to her warriors, the globe amplifying her voice. "Princess wants them," she said. She touched the net with her spear. It fell apart, the meshes crumbling like burnt

17

matchsticks.

"I'm *tired*," Boo announced. "I must be *carried*. I'll ride on a man. That man."

"OK," said the Warrior Queen. The warrior swooped Boo onto his shoulders. The party moved off in the direction from which it had come.

When it reached the place where the Doop had fallen and died, the party stopped. There were extravagant howlings and lamentations, in which the Queen joined, her face a mask of agony, her body torturing itself to death.

Then – snap! – it was over and apparently forgotten: the party walked on again. Some warriors still pranced and made warlike sounds. Most simply walked. Mina and Leo, silent at first, talked.

"That boss-woman said 'Princess'," Mina said. "What did *that* mean?"

"Don't ask me. No idea."

"And all that howling and carrying-on over the dead Doop: what was all that about? Why do it twice?"

Leo said, "Ah. That's interesting. I've got a theory about that."

"You've always got a theory," Mina said.

But then two Doops came and stared at them. Leo stared back. "*Collarbones*!" Leo said, out of the corner of his mouth.

Mina saw what he had seen: in the hollows above the collarbones of both Doops, there were little grilles – covered slots. The perforated mesh or grill covering the slots seemed to be of factory-made stuff – but, no, it must have been animal tissue because, as Mina watched, one of the Doops closed his grille. It seemed to "grow" shut.

"Control systems?" she said to Leo. "Sensory organs? Communications? What?"

Leo shrugged. Probably all three, and half a dozen more, he thought. After Man, Doops could be the cleverest, most complicated two-legged beings in the Galaxy. Too complicated to be what their designers had intended them to be.

Boo rode by on the shoulders of a warrior Doop. "Faster!" he commanded. "Do proper running!" The warrior ran. He did not sweat or breathe heavily. Yet he ran so fast that the child's reddish-brown curls bobbed about on his head with every stride.

"The other Doops," Mina said quietly. "Just look at them!"

Leo looked and saw something strange. The Doop carrying Boo ran in a weaving pattern, steered by Boo. The main body of the Doops had been walking.

But now many of the other Doops began imitating the one carrying Boo! Solemn-faced and warlike, they trotted, swerved, circled, wove in and out of each other. Even the Warrior Queen, still carried by two males, was being thrown about on their shoulders. Yet she issued no orders and her expression was unchanged.

"Ants?" Mina asked Leo.

He understood what she meant. "Ants," he agreed. "Behaving blindly. Imitating each other. Conditioned reflexes. See a dead Doop – do a ritual mourning ceremony. One does it, they all do it. Just like ants."

Now all the Doops were at it! – and Boo was laughing out loud, delighted with himself. "Silly," he shouted. "More! Gee up!"

The Doops carrying the Warrior Queen were the first to collapse. The grilled vents in their collarbones gaped wide. Noises came from their mouths, noises that Mina and Leo heard as "Pow! Pow!" The carriers stumbled, legs buckling. They fell forward. The Queen slid from their shoulders, gracefully and effortlessly. All around her, Doops stumbled to their knees, went down on all fours, or simply laid down. Yet no face showed distress.

"Pow," they said. "Pow, pow, pow."

The Warrior Queen unhurriedly stretched, adjusted her jewellery – and spoke into her golden sphere. Mina and Leo thought they heard her say, "Pow." Boo came to them. "Make them go again," he ordered. "Make them be horses."

Mina said, "Later, Boo."

"No, now, I want *now*." He stuck out his lower lip and looked at the Doops. "All lying the same way," he said.

Leo said, "He's right! Look, Mina – they've all pointed themselves in the same direction. All facing over there. And their grille things are open. Why?"

There seemed no answer. They had halted in what was almost a clearing: a place still crowded with ugly undergrowth and "trees" that were not trees; but there was a view through the tree trunks. They studied the view.

"No birds, no animals," Leo said. "No insects, even."

"Oh, there'll be insects," Mina said, dully. "Really nasty ones. Slimy ones, creepy-crawly ones. It's that sort of place. Yuck!"

"The manual said not." Leo's eyes were taking in everything: the dank, miserable sky, the shabby hills and ridges, the spear-like crowns of the trees, motionless. No wind, no bright sun. He thought, We humans

20

certainly found a mean, rotten little planet on which to dump the Doops.

"One single, solitary mountain," he said to Mina, pointing it out.

"That's hardly a mountain, it's just a lump," Mina said. She jabbed one of the purple leaves at her feet with a blade of her all-purpose knife. Sticky, milky, greenish fluid bulged out, much the same colour as the sky. She made a disgusted noise and stared at the mountain. It was perhaps a kilometre away. It was dark, but had shades of copper and purple here and there. "At least the mountain's *unique*," she said, bitterly, "I mean, there's nothing else like it that I can see. As if I cared."

"It's what all the Doops have lined themselves up with," Leo said. "They're all facing it. With their grille things wide open."

"So they have, you observant boy," Mina said. "How ab—so—lute—ly, earth-shatteringly interesting." She stuck her knife into every plant in reach.

"Mina's cross," Boo said. He got off her lap and sat on Leo's.

Leo thought, I don't blame her. It's all just hitting her. But it will be all right in the end, won't it? Ma and Da will come back for us when they get the ship sorted out. They've probably fixed it already, although...

So many things had gone wrong all at once. First the touchdown. "Touchdown" was a laugh. Crash, wallop, skid, thump, screech, BANG. Some touchdown. Only half the ship's gear had worked. The Holdoff wouldn't hold off, the Comm hadn't communicated for days and days, the Navvy unit seldom navigated. The whole ship was a disaster.

21

Well, hired ships often were. Ma and Da never had enough money, they never seemed to find their Aladdin's Cave. They just went on and on, bashing through the Galaxy, always smiling and optimistic, never letting on to the children. As if the children couldn't guess!

And now, Leo thought, here we are in lovely Argosy IV where there ought to be beryllium or teryllium or some rare stuff worth millions and millions back on Earth. But of course, there won't be. There never has been and there never will be.

Ma and Da thought we three were still in the ship but we weren't, we'd craftily deserted the ship. We wanted to feel, just for a minute or two, solid ground under our feet; and to breathe some real air...

And then, using its very last full-boost reserves, the ship had lifted off. Soared into the wild blue yonder. With its boosters belching black and yellow smoke, its rear end wagging like a dog's and its main drives making noises like twenty-seven car crashes. Gone without us.

Hopeless.

But, no, you must never give up hope. Da is always saying that. I wonder what he's saying this moment? And where he's saying it?

I wonder if they're able to say anything at all? No, don't think that. Never give up hope. Da and Ma say so.

And then, with the complete suddenness with which the Doops seemed to do everything, the warriors were on their feet and the Warrior Queen was lifted aloft on some broad shoulders, and they were on the move again.

Pretty Pig Princess

They reached the town, or the village. The place where the Doops lived. There were houses. The houses were familiar to Leo and Mina: they were simply Gala-Freight packing cases and containers. The Doops had stacked some of them and spaced out the others. They had knocked holes in the sides for doors and windows.

"Hutches," Mina said. Leo glanced at her. Her mouth was tight, her neck taut, her eyes lowered.

They came to a curving rock-face and followed the curve. The Doops had dug deeply into the rock here and there. Obviously they had tools – Earth-style tools, probably laser cutters.

Some of the holes had to be Doop dwellings, for Leo saw pin-ups. The pin-ups were reproductions of the old

Doop press advertisements: smiling humans, attentive Doops ready to serve. He spotted a pile of bright orange and black Doop manuals, the books you got when you bought a Doop. The manuals were crammed with operating instructions, service agencies' addresses and special offers. Now they were curling at the edges: relics of ancient history.

The curving rock-face took a still sharper curve; and revealed the Palace.

It was splendid. There was a fountain with dolphins and a little boy who should have blown water through the shell he held to his lips. But there was no water.

There was a courtyard with Greek pillars, Spanish arches and trellis-work to hold up vines and roses. But there were no vines or roses.

There was a ceremonial entrance – a great arch topped by a coat of arms over a massive door with studded gilt panelling. Such an entrance deserved guards: and there they were, two Doops dressed as Roman Centurions. They stood motionless, chins high, chests proud, legs rigid, spears at the ready.

"Fibreglass," Leo whispered. "Everything's fibreglass, even the guards' armour."

The Warrior Queen turned warning eyes on them. Before she could speak, the golden sphere in her hand sounded a musical chime followed by an ascending run of bell-like notes.

"Kneel, she is coming!" said the Warrior Queen. The Doops all knelt.

"Kneel!" the Warrior Queen told the three Earth-siders. Unwillingly, they went down on their knees.

The great door creaked and began to open. "Bow!" commanded the Warrior Queen. The heads of the Doops bowed to the ground. The bell-like notes sounded louder from the golden sphere.

Framed in the door, there appeared a girl of Mina's age. A fairy-tale princess.

She was the prettiest girl ever seen. Her face glowed with an angel softness. Her spun-gold hair fell to her waist. Adorable curling tendrils escaped to frame her cheeks and violet-blue eyes. The perfect curves of her rose-petal mouth were slightly parted to reveal pearl-like teeth.

Her dress was of heavy damasks over gem-encrusted, luminous, pale silks and satins. One little foot, slippered and buckled, peeped out beneath the heavy folds of her skirts. Ruffed lace, infinitely fine, set off the even finer texture of her neck. A tiny coronet, alive with bright diamonds and dark pearls, nestled on top of her golden head.

Her long-lashed eyes gently surveyed the three wide-eyed humans.

She spoke.

"I am the Princess," she said, in a voice more musical even than the chimes from the sphere. The humans could find nothing to say.

"I am the Princess," she repeated. "Who," she continued, "who in hell are you?"

The Warrior Queen, still kneeling, began to tell the story of the chase and capture. The Princess cut her short with a wave of her pretty little hand. "You go on and on," she said in her honey-sweet voice. "*You* bore me, *they* bore me. I thought I wanted them. Now I don't, because they're boring."

"But, Your Majesty, you told me —" began the Warrior Queen.

"Never mind that. You should have known that I wouldn't like them. If you'd brought me creatures with fur and claws, or fins and tails, I'd have been interested. But these are just ordinary and boring. Just humans."

"Shall I dispose of them, Your Majesty?"

"Of course. Take them away and break them."

"Yes, Your Majesty."

"No, wait..." The Princess fixed her long-lashed eyes on Mina. "Perhaps I want *this* one, the girl one, after all. Yes, I do want her. Get rid of the other two, the boys."

"Immediately, Your —"

"No, wait... I want them *all*. They are to be given whatever they need, do you understand?"

"I'm *hungry*," Boo said, looking trustfully at the Princess.

She answered with the great rope of pearls loosely wrapped round her right wrist. The hand lifted, the pearls swung. They slashed across Boo's face.

"Whatever they need," the Princess repeated as she turned on her heel and floated away.

Mina shouted, "You... You filthy...!" and tried to run after her. A Doop seized her arms and effortlessly held her back. Leo comforted Boo. His face was only lightly marked. "Pig lady!" he said.

"It's all right, Boo," Leo said.

"It's *not* all right. Hitting people." He began his boo noise. Leo soothed him and prevented him from crying.

After a time, Boo said, "She is pretty, isn't she?"

"Yes, Boo, very pretty."

"Pretty pig lady," Boo said, rubbing the bruises on his face. "Pretty piggy, piggy, piggy pretty."

*   *   *

Mina was taken to the Princess's apartments. Leo had been right: the Italianate decorations, the French furniture, the Renaissance plasterwork – all were fakes and fibreglass.

Mina settled herself on a tapestried chair whose tapestry designs were merely printed. She wondered who had ordered this fake splendour, and why. The voice of the Princess interrupted her thoughts. "Stand up!" she said. Mina stood up, taking her time. The Princess noticed the insult. The bracelet of pearls swung at her just as it had at Boo. Mina raised her arm. The pearls burst their threaded links and scattered like gunshot. "Pick them up, every one of them," said the Princess.

"I won't," Mina said.

"Then you shall be beaten," said the Princess. "Beaten twice. First, for sitting down when I am standing. Second, for breaking my bracelet."

"I never broke your stupid bracelet —"

"And again for not calling me 'Your Majesty'."

"You can't beat me. You shan't. You don't beat girls."

"You don't beat girls, *Your Majesty*. Say it or you shall be beaten four times."

Mina was stunned.

"I would like to see you beaten," said the Princess. "It would be something new. Beaten four times. One, two, three, four." She sounded girlish and charming.

Mina thought, That Doop who held me... his hands were cold, there was strength in them but no warm life. Was there death in them? Surely not. They can't kill animals and birds because there aren't any. They can't kill each other because they can't afford deaths. They can't kill humans or even harm them because they're programed not to. Or *are* they? If only I could find out...

"You can't beat girls," she told the Princess; then quickly added, "Your Majesty."

"Can't I? Why not?"

"You just *can't*. It – it isn't done. *Because* they're girls, Your Majesty."

The Princess thought about this for some time. Then she clapped her little hands, smiled radiantly and said, "Of *course* not! I understand now! Because of the babies inside them! Of course, of course!"

Mina's mind skidded wildly.

"I shall beat that boy instead," the Princess said. "The big one. Is the little one your son?"

Again Mina's mind skidded. "No, he's my brother. Like the big one. Both my brothers."

"*Your Majesty*," said the Princess.

"Both my brothers, Your Majesty."

"Ah, brothers and sisters," said the Princess. "Many humans have those... And you humans eat food, don't you? And drink drinks?"

"Oh, yes, Your Majesty! My little brother must have food, he's very hungry."

The Princess smiled with genuine sweetness. "We don't have food or drink," she said. "We don't use them. So I can't give you any. Do you mind?"

"But, Your Majesty! We'll *die*!"

Immediately the Princess's lovely little face changed. It twisted with anger and fear. "Don't say that!" she cried. "Don't *dare* say that! I shall beat him for that! Beat him and beat him!"

"Your Majesty, I don't understand... Beat *who*?"

"Your brother. The big one. Because you said that word. That wicked word!"

"What word, Your Majesty? Do you mean 'die'?"

"Ah!" shouted the Princess. "You dreadful thing! You... You... Oh, the wickedness!"

She ran to the bell rope in the corner of the room and tugged at it. Two Centurion Doops appeared. "Beat him!" cried the Princess. "The boy, the big one — take him to the courtyard, tie him up, beat him and beat him! I shall tell you how!" She turned her face, twisted with spite, to Mina and said, "I know how it's done. *Exactly* how it's done. I have read books, seen pictures, oh yes! You shall watch, you shall see! Come!"

As if locked within a nightmare, Mina followed the Princess to the courtyard.

In the courtyard, the preparations for the whipping were almost but not quite complete. It was Boo who held up the proceedings.

He had, all on his own, found a supply of food.

His treasure-trove was one wall of a Doop house. The house was made of Mark VII bulkhead pressings taken from an Earthside ship's motor shield; aluminium container lids from a long-forgotten delivery from Earthside; and a stack of hermetically sealed packs of foods and drinks, left behind some ten years ago by human visitors from Earthside.

Boo recognized the packs at once. They were much the same as those carried by Ma and Da on their various ships. "I want those," he told the Doop householder. "I need them." He tugged at the heavy packs.

The Doop said, "OK," and carried them effortlessly, three at a time, to the courtyard of the Palace. The Doop house collapsed to one side but the Doop appeared not to mind.

When Boo, pink-faced with happy anticipation, tore open the first pack, there was great excitement among the Doops. They should have been setting the stage for Leo's whipping; instead they clustered round Boo.

"Stew, oh yes," he announced, holding up a Thermopak for all to see. He made his quiet, greedy noise – "Ymm, ymm, ymm," – as he ripped the right-tab off the Thermopak and released the aroma of hot beef stew.

A plastic spoon came with each Thermopak. The spoon carried stew to his mouth. His mouth opened and the stew went into it. The stew was then "vanished", as if by a conjurer, to make way for another spoonful.

The Doops were amazed by this performance. Some talked among themselves in low tones. Others craned forward over Boo's seated body, following the sequence of spoon to Thermopak, spoon to mouth, food in mouth, food gone. Gone *where*? their wondering faces seemed to ask.

When Leo joined Boo's feast, their amazement was boundless. Leo had spotted a Thermopak of a favourite food. Whole asparagus. He held each long stalk above his mouth, said "Mmm, great!" and somehow caused the long stalk to slide into himself and vanish for ever. He did this again and again. Each time, the Doops' wondering appreciation increased. Had they been humans, they would have applauded.

Even the Warrior Queen squatted on her haunches and watched entranced.

But then the Princess and Mina arrived. The sideshow was over. The main event was about to begin.

Under the Princess's instructions, one Doop placed

himself on all fours on the ground. Two more seized Leo's arms. Two more held his ankles. They held his body face-down over the kneeling Doop.

Mina started forward and screamed, "No! No!" A Doop grabbed her and held her, stifling her screams with a long forearm. Boo ran round in panicky circles, crying, "What will they *do*?" No one bothered with him.

The Princess seated herself on a throne, her dimpled chin cupped in her hand. "Start the whipping!" she commanded the Warrior Queen.

"Yes, Your Majesty. But *how*, Your Majesty? What with?"

The question stopped everything. Nobody had considered it. The Princess herself found the solution: she rose to her feet and tore off the sash that circled her waist. "This, use *this*!" she said and flung the sash at the Warrior Queen.

The whipping began.

The sash was lifted high in the Warrior Queen's splendid, muscular arm. It flailed down on Leo's back. A low murmur came from the assembled Doops. The Doop who held Mina was so fascinated that he let her go. She ran to her brother Leo and knelt by him.

He turned his head and winked at her. "Morons," he whispered, and gave a secret grin.

"More whipping!" the Princess shouted. "Much more!" Again the Warrior Queen lifted her arms. Again the whip came down on Leo's back.

His shoulders began to heave. He was laughing. Mina, too, found it hard not to giggle. The Princess's sash was of velvet, backed with some soft material. A blow from it might have hurt a fly. Or it might not.

"Stop laughing!" Mina whispered in Leo's ear.

31

"I can't!"

"You must! Pretend it hurts! Make noises – groans, stuff like that!"

"I'll try. Tell Boo it's all play-acting."

"More whipping!" cried the Princess. "Take the girl away!"

Mina was seized. She rolled her eyes, struggled to escape, made pathetic noises. Boo ran to her, his eyes wide and anxious. She pulled a special face at him, squinting her eyes horribly and muttering, "Con!" He understood at once. His face relaxed.

The whipping went on. Mina thoroughly enjoyed it, but perhaps not as much as Leo. His groans were awful, heart-rending. He developed a particularly good pathetic howl, a wavering "Whooo-hooo-hooooo!" that ran up and down the scale.

Perhaps this sound was too much for the Princess's prettily shaped ears. "Enough!" she commanded. The Warrior Queen stepped back. The Doops released Leo.

The Princess stood close to him examining his face. "Was it a proper beating?" she asked. "Did it hurt?"

"Oh yes! Like anything!" Leo replied.

The Princess turned to Mina, whose face dripped real tears – she had always been able to make herself weep. "It's supposed to hurt, isn't it?" the Princess asked.

"Definitely, Your Majesty," Mina replied.

"So we did it properly?"

"Oh, yes. It was a very good whipping."

"How nice," said the Princess. "We must do it again. Your brother is a good whipping boy, like the ones they had in the old days, centuries ago. I know all about it, of course. I know millions of things."

"I'm sure you do, Your Majesty."

"Yes. Whenever I do anything wrong, we shall have a whipping to punish me. I must think of wrong things to do."

Boo's furious face thrust up at them. "But it was all a *con*!" he complained.

Mina smiled and clamped her hand over his mouth. "Quite right, Boo," she said. "It was all a – a *con*siderable success."

"Good. Now I will show you my dresses," the Princess said to Mina.

Supa Loo

"These are my dresses," said the Princess. "All of them. All mine."

Looking at her glowing, delicately beautiful face and hearing her childlike voice, Mina could have kissed her. Thinking of her treatment of Boo and Leo, she could have killed her. Mina sat on the edge of the Princess's sumptuous bed and gazed blankly in front of her, trying to make sense of things.

"Yes, I have a bed," the Princess said, patting the soft satin quilt. This remark, too, baffled Mina. So she has a bed, Mina thought. Well, just fancy that. Hurray for you. Next she'll tell me she has a WC.

"And this is the lavatory, *my* lavatory," the Princess said, throwing open an ivory and gilt door. "Look! It

35

has a WC!" She pointed to it. Mina looked at it. The bowl was decorated with gold-leaf patterns. The gold looked genuine.

"It must have cost a fortune," was all Mina could say.

"Oh, yes. It did. Everything I have is of the very best, from Earthside. Of course, I never actually use the WC."

Mina gulped and said, "Well... What *do* you use, Your Majesty?"

But the Princess only said, "Why do you keep calling me Your Majesty? I *hate* 'Your Majesty'. You are my very best friend, you must call me by my real name."

Oh, so now I am your very best friend, Mina thought. Well, well. Aloud, she said, "What name shall I call you by?"

"S–u–p–a," the Princess answered. "Supa. Do you like it? I like it."

"It's lovely," Mina said. In her mind, pennies dropped and questions started answering themselves. Supa! Of course: just the sort of joke that Earthside technologists and boffins *would* make! The Princess was a Doop: a very superior Doop. Therefore, Supa-Doop, super-dooper. Very funny, ha-ha.

"Everything I have is special," the Princess said over her shoulder. She was holding dresses in front of her, one after another, admiring her reflection in a gilt pedestal mirror.

"Of course, Your Maj—, I mean, Supa," Mina replied. "Everything must be special because *you* are so special...?"

"Yes, that's right. *Unique.*" She gazed solemnly into Mina's eyes and added, "I'm the One-off. The only one of my kind. You wanna know something? I'm a very special little lady, you know that?" She spoke the last words in an accurate American accent. "They broke the mould when they'd made me," she said, nodding her head solemnly.

Mina said, "They. Who were *they*? Can you remember?"

The Princess turned away and said, "This oyster satin: sometimes I think it is my favourite dress for formal occasions. But I'm never sure."

Mina thought, Ah: that's her programing, her conditioning. Even if she knew the answer to my question – who were *they*? – she could never speak. Because *they*, her makers, wouldn't allow her to. Her memory circuits would cut out. Her chips or tapes, or whatever she has inside her, would go blank.

The Princess said, "I did enjoy the whipping, didn't you?"

Mina said, "Yes and no. It was a perfect whipping, of course; just right. But Leo is my brother."

"Oh, boys don't matter," said the Princess. "Boys are males. Who cares about males?"

"Yes, I see that," Mina said, waiting for more.

"It's the same with Earthside bees," the Princess said. "They kill off the males, the drones, don't they? And serve them right."

"I didn't know that," Mina lied. "Why do they kill off the males?"

"Because they don't have *babies*, stupid! I thought *you* would have known that, coming from Earthside."

"Silly of me," Mina said. Now she was floundering again; the pennies in her mind had stopped dropping.

"You'll let me see Leo?" she said.

"Oh, yes, of course. If he hasn't been broken." She adjusted the golden tendrils of hair round her ears.

"No, wait, I haven't *ordered* him broken, so he must be around somewhere. Do you like this silver and green robe? I do, sometimes. Do you want to go and find your brother?" She was very busy with the robe.

"Oh, yes please, Your Majesty."

"That's right, you should always call me, 'Your Majesty'. One day I will let you call me by my real name, Supa. S–u–p–a. Do you like it? *I* like it."

Now the Princess was trying on hats. Each hat suited her better than the last.

Mina left her and went in search of Leo.

Leo was tied up inside a typical Doop hovel, guarded by two male Doop sentries. He looked pathetic.

"Oh, hello," he said. "Welcome to my kennel. How are things in the Palace?"

"Oh, Leo...!"

"Oh, Leo!" he mimicked, bitterly. Then, "At least I've had plenty to eat and drink. Because of Boo. He's been trotting back and forth bringing me all kinds of goodies. He even pats my head."

"What are they doing with him?"

"Nothing much. They're not interested in him, he's so small. I suppose they see him as a kind of walking doll. How are you getting on with Her Royal Highness? Still chums? You'd better be. Then you can protect Boo."

"Shall I undo those ropes?"

"No, it's not worth the hassle. I've undone them myself two or three times – they don't know how to tie knots – but they always notice and tie me up all over again."

"Oh, Leo...!"

"Yes, well, you said that before. This time, say something intelligent."

"All right. Tell me about Doops and the Princess."

"If you'd bother to *attend* at school – to look at the *serious* TV programmes —"

"All right, all right, I'm ignorant. All I know is that Doops were manufactured by Earthside scientists to act as super-efficient, all-purpose, human-looking, robot servants. But they were a failure because —"

"Because they proved to be too clever by half," Leo said, "which is not really surprising. I mean, if a Doop's made clever enough to do everything *you* want done, you mustn't be surprised if it goes and does something *it* wants done."

"A girl at school," Mina said, "had a Doop – her parents did, I mean – and it was terrific for months on end. Then, one day, the mother – she was stinking rich, otherwise they couldn't have afforded a Doop in the first place – had lots of her friends round for tea. And she told the Doop, 'Oh, do make *lots* of tea, *lashings* of it, won't you, there's a dear?' And the Doop gave her a funny look. Then —"

Leo said, "Everyone knows that story. The Doop gave the woman a funny look and went into the kitchen and made enough tea to fill a swimming pool."

"Well, you might have let me finish —"

"And then there were all the stories about Doops smothering babies and the Doop who couldn't fit the car into the garage so he just smashed it back and forth until the garage fitted the car."

"Do you think the stories were all true?" Mina said.

"Enough of them, anyway. Doops getting stroppy, Doops getting cunning and malicious, Doops getting too big for their boots, which is why they had to pack it in. First they banned the sale of Doops, then all the ones that were left were packed off to this place. Exiled."

"Why here?"

"Well, I suppose because Argosy IV suited the Doops' needs. Right environment and ecology and so on. But there's another good reason I can guess."

"What?"

"Look – the inventors of the Doops wouldn't want all their work destroyed, would they? I mean, Doops were a *product*, something you'd sell for a profit. Just because the product wasn't right first time, you wouldn't give up, would you? You'd find out what was wrong with the Mark I models and hope to do better with the Mark II. So the inventors would agree to get rid of the Doops; but they'd make sure they were sent to a remote, unpopular place, where they could still be *reached*. For further research and development. Nobody visits Argosy IV if they can avoid it so this place would be fine. The boffins could work, secretly, on their improved Mark II."

"Mark II, the super Doop," Mina said. Then, "Would you like to know the Princess's real name?"

"Not particularly. Why?"

"Her real name is S–u–p–a. *Supa*."

Leo stared at Mina. He said, "You mean, she's *it*? The new, improved, double-whammy, state-of-the-art, Mark II Doop?"

"She must be. Supa-Doop. I mean, she's a huge improvement. She talks better, moves better and she's got a colossal information back-up built into her. I've been with her, I know."

Leo fiddled with his bonds and said, "No, wait a minute. She's not perfect because she's *too* perfect. They wouldn't want to market her. She's too beautiful!

40

Imagine having something like that around the house, day after day, never growing older, never changing! She'd drive her owners mad. Particularly the women."

Mina thought about this. "You're right," she said at last. "Do you know what she is? She's a one-off work of art, a special, a collector's piece."

"But whose collection?" Leo said. "What collector?"

Boo appeared in the gap that served as a doorway. "Their swords aren't sharp," he complained. "All *blunt*. I think the Doops are stupid. Look – cola drink!"

Leo got free of his bonds. The three of them drank ten-year-old colas. They tasted as good as new.

The Doop guards tied Leo up. He kept his wrists expanded and rigid and untied himself. They tied him up again. He escaped again.

Night came. The greenish sky of Argosy IV turned to dark mud and the night rains splattered dismally over the uncaring guards. Leo considered his position:

1. He would live. He would not starve. Boo would bring him food and drink.

2. Boo was safe. The Doops did not wish or need to hurt him. At this moment, he was probably sleeping with or near Mina.

3. Mina was all right, unless the Princess took a dislike to her. Apparently the Princess's thoughts and moods changed from minute to minute. But Mina was clever. Mina could handle her.

4. The Doops were not killers. The hunt had been just play-acting, a ritual play, probably invented by the Warrior Queen to keep the Doops' mind-mechanisms occupied. Was the Warrior Queen a threat? No, she obeyed the Princess.

41

5. *I can't go on like this much longer.*

Thought No. 5 was the one that mattered. Leo made a mental list of the things that might help him and the others escape, or seize power, or do *something*. The list was disappointing.

He had on his person a luminous watch: a twentieth-century clockwork machine with a luminous dial — a treasured, useless antique; a standard-issue knife with eleven blades and tools; a proper, twenty-first century, standard-issue watch with calculator, memories and a dozen other functions; radio, contained in the watch — a complete two-way communications system. Using it, he had already tried many times to reach his parents' ship, without a glimmer of success. This did not surprise him.

His main items of clothing were standard-issue boots and a standard-issue undersuit. When he and the others had sneaked off the ship, they had no time for helmets or Viro suits. This could turn out to be a pity: the suits and helmets offered various kinds of services and protections. Still, Argosy IV was not a truly hostile place.

He also carried 22.3 Units in mixed coins, a broken haircomb and his lucky charm, a baby doll made of veined crystal from the planet Traskon.

He had no paper tissues, no toothbrush, no soap.

And, Leo thought, no hope. But things would change, they had to change...

He put his watch very close to his eyes so that its glimmering lights filled his eye and mind, consoling him. I'm not going to be that Princess's whipping boy for much longer, he told himself. Not on your life.

He slept.

Mina told the Princess, "I must sleep." The Princess

said, "Oh yes! Do! I shall watch!"

Mina thought, Of course; she doesn't sleep. She doesn't need to. What does she do instead? I think I remember: Doops go into rundown, an eighty per cent switch-off. Or something like that.

"Go on, sleep!" the Princess ordered. She leaned over Mina and peered into her eyes. Mina yawned — she was very tired — and laughed. "I can't just go to sleep — bang — like that!" she said.

Boo put his head round the door of the Princess's bedroom. "I'm not tired," he said. "I'm *never* tired." His eyes were pink and puffy with exhaustion. "So you needn't say good-night to me," he said.

This was a hint. Mina kissed and cuddled him. "Lie down, anyway," she said.

"But I'm not tired."

"Of course you're not. But let's pretend you are."

His bed was the Princess's quilt. Mina tucked him in. He was asleep before Mina finished. The Princess watched everything.

"Is that all?" she said. "Is that falling asleep?"

"Yes, that's it."

"Wake him up and make him do it again."

"I can't, Your Majesty, you just — don't."

"But there was nothing interesting to see. *You* do it. Go on! You took some clothes off. Why? I shall do the same."

Mina lay down on the bed, closed her eyes and pretended to be asleep. She tried to make plans but could not concentrate. She heard clinks and jingles as the Princess removed her jewellery; then the sound of a small object falling — and a crunch — and the Princess shouting, "Oh! Oh! Stupid, bad!"

Mina sat up and saw that the Princess had dropped a

bracelet, then trodden on it.

"Stupid, wicked!" cried the Princess. "I shall whip him for this! Whip him and whip him!"

Mina lay back, closed her eyes and lay sleepless.

Mina slept at last – only to be awakened by the Voice of Doom. The voice came from Boo, who loomed over her like a pale ghost in the darkness of the Princess's bedroom.

"*The water's coming*," he said, in his deepest foghorn tones.

Mina started up and looked wildly about her. There was no water to be seen. No tank had burst, no flood was sweeping through the Palace. She said, "What...? What...? Boo – What...?" But he had already vanished. The door to the Princess's lavatory opened; there was a trickling sound; then a cascade as the wc was flushed.

Boo reappeared. "Better now," he said.

Mina heard the quilt rustle as Boo pulled it over himself and his contented murmuring, "Ymm, ymm, ymm." Then silence, as he settled down to deep sleep.

For Mina, sleep was out of the question. She was completely awake. She got out of the wide, soft bed and sat on its edge for some time, feeling her pulse settle down. She walked to the window and drew aside the heavy brocade curtains. It was raining outside, lightly. The glowering sky was not completely dark and seemed to lighten as she watched it. Oh well, she thought, dawn would happen quickly on such a small planet.

She would talk with the Princess. But where was she? Gone. Obviously the Princess did not need sleep. She could be anywhere, doing whatever Doops do at night.

44

In that case, Mina decided, I can explore the Palace. Where are the light switches? There didn't seem to be any. Perhaps Doops could see in the dark?

She felt cold and threw a beautiful fringed shawl belonging to the Princess over her shoulders. She tiptoed past the sleeping Boo and stifled a giggle that rose in her throat. "'The water's coming,' indeed!"

She discovered, not to her surprise, that the Palace was small, elaborate and mostly phoney. It was a toy, nothing more, made of fake materials, plastics, spray-on gilding, glass that turned out to be plastic and woods that turned out to be extruded something or other. Some of the Princess's possessions were real and valuable; most of the Palace was rubbish. As the dawn light grew brighter, everything she saw and touched grew tawdrier.

She became impatient with the sham grandeur and walked through a huge, over-decorated, flimsy door leading from the banqueting room to the courtyard. There were Doops on guard. They held magnificent spears or halberds. They crossed their spears to bar her way and looked fierce.

"Oh, don't be silly," Mina said, and pushed the spears aside. Their points felt rubbery and blunt. The Doops took up their former on-guard positions. They made no attempt actually to stop her.

She walked on, seeing the gritty surface underfoot merge into the dull undergrowth; even the "grounds" of the Palace did not extend far. There were Doops here and there. They seemed neither asleep nor awake. They were posed, like statues. After a time, Mina noticed that all their collarbone grilles were wide open; and that each Doop's head and body was turned in the same direction – towards the mountain.

It was a dull walk... She decided to turn back but noticed a big drum or chimneypot, perhaps three metres across, sticking out of the ground. It looked like an Earthside object. A vent? A chimney? Something of the sort, because it was hollow. She leaned over the edge and looked down. There was little to be seen but darkness. But she could just make out a coarse mesh screen or barrier.

She lost interest and continued her walk, thinking, Leo should be somewhere over there. Perhaps the Princess is with him?

Then she smelt coffee.

At first, she thought nothing of the smell. The smell of coffee was the smell of her own and a million other homes on any Earthside morning. But, wait! Coffee on Argosy IV? Whose coffee?

She sniffed the air. The smell could come only from over *there*...

She followed her nose. It led her back to the big chimney. She stood over it, sniffing. There could be no mistake: the smell of coffee, real coffee, freshly made, came from it.

She shouted down into the blackness. "Hi! Anybody there?"

No answer.

She shouted again. "Coffee, I can smell coffee! Who's there?"

No answer.

And then the Princess stood beside her. "You are not allowed here," she said. "You are not allowed anywhere without my permission. Your brother shall be whipped for this!"

"Two whippings in one morning?" Mina said, sarcastically.

46

"As many whippings as I choose! All at the same time!" the Princess answered.

Mina managed not to laugh.

Later that morning, Leo was ceremonially whipped once again. The Doop guards paraded, the Princess wore a different dress and a glittering coronet. Everything should have been perfect. But the occasion began badly.

Plainly, the Princess was bored. She had seen one whipping and was not thrilled by the repeat performance. Leo, too, was not at his best. He was tired after an uncomfortable night; and his breakfast of tomato soup and cola disagreed with him. He had the hiccups.

"Shout! Yell! Suffer!" Mina hissed at him. Leo was, as before, horsed on the back of the Doop. Mina placed herself beside him, where she could display sisterly grief. "Oh, my poor brother!" she cried, wringing her hands. "Oh, the agony! (*Suffer*, you fool!) Oh, the pain!" The Princess nodded approvingly but obviously expected something more.

She got what she wanted when tufts of Leo's uncombed hair became trapped in the armour of the Doop supporting him. The Doop was on all fours, Leo was tied over the Doop's bent back. The Doop arched his back and plates of armour closed like a vice. "My hair!" Leo shouted. He began struggling.

The velvet sash rose and fell – Leo struggled – the Doop braced himself more firmly than ever. Leo howled and hiccuped in genuine agony. "My hair, you're pulling it out!" he cried. Real tears ran down his cheeks. Having one's hair pulled stimulates the tear glands.

Mina, seeing what was happening, enjoyed herself.

"Oh, dearest brother!" she howled. "Lift your poor head! Look into my eyes!" Leo could do neither, of course.

The whipping continued. The Princess enjoyed it almost as much as Mina. Boo cried, "Do some more!" and beamed.

Leo hiccuped and swore.

When the whipping was over, Mina should have gone with Leo to his kennel. She should have said, "Look, I couldn't help laughing. I really am sorry, please forgive me." She should have brought him luxuries from the Princess's bedroom and drink to soothe his hiccups.

She meant to do all these things; but the Princess said, in her friendliest voice, "Come with me, Mina. I have many more dresses. I shall let you try them and look at yourself in my mirror."

Mina forgot Leo and went with the Princess.

The dresses were exciting and beautiful. They were made of fine and genuine Earthside materials. There were dresses of many periods – Georgian, Victorian, new-Elizabethan (Mina particularly liked the 100-year-old mini-skirt style) and present-day, twenty-first century fashions.

"Ah, this one is late Victorian," the Princess said, "with a bustle and everything! Try it on."

Mina, struggling into the dress, said, "How do you know so much about everything, Your Majesty?"

"You may call me Supa. Oh, I know *everything*. Test me if you like. Go on, ask me questions."

Mina asked her dozens of questions. If the questions were about facts, the Princess answered them without hesitation. Mina thought, What a terrific programing job they did on her! They must have stuffed whole encyclopaedia into her memories!

But the Princess was also astonishingly ignorant. When Mina ran out of questions, the Princess took over. "When," she said, "are you going to have a baby?"

"Oh, I don't know..." Mina replied. As she adjusted the dress, she thought about the future. Would she have many boyfriends? Would she ever truly fall in love? What sort of man would she marry, in how many years' time?

The Princess interrupted her thoughts. "Have a baby now," she said. "Go on! I command you! Have a baby! I want to see! And I want to hold it and dress it and love it and everything!"

Mina kept her eyes on her reflection in the mirror. She did not want to look at the Princess because there was something in her voice – wistfulness, sadness, a childish hopelessness – that was frightening. For the first time, Mina felt pity for the lovely toy leaning towards her, touching her human arm with inhumanly perfect fingers.

You poor thing, – yes, *thing* – Mina thought. They've filled you to overflowing with memories, logics back-ups, responses and all the rest of it; then left you dangling. You know and feel so much that you must have more. The other Doops are just advanced robots. But you – you are more than half-way to being human...

"A baby," the Princess said. She was standing so close to Mina that her reflection crowded the mirror. Mina's eyes seemed to be drawn to hers. "Go on," the Princess whispered. "A baby! A baby!"

Mina tried to break away. The Princess caught her arm. "Please!" she said. "Show me! I must know!" Her grip was as strong as steel. "I don't want just to *stop*," she said, in the voice of a lost child.

Mina turned her back on the Princess and tried to stop the tears coming. But they came.

Later, Mina visited Leo. "Nice of you to call," he said. "Slumming again?"

Mina tossed cushions, bedding, toilet paper, food and drinks at him. "It's not *my* fault," she stormed. "I got *trapped*. By *her*."

"Oh, you mean Her Gracious Majesty," Leo said. "Nasty little cow. I'd like to short-circuit her works and watch her fizzle out!"

Immediately, Mina's storm was over. "Fizzle out," she said, quietly. "That's what she's afraid of. Fizzling out. She *knows* about herself, Leo."

"I know about her, too," Leo said. "She's a vicious robot toy. Having me *whipped* . . ."

"All right, she's what you say. But she's also something else. I can't help being sorry for her. She's doomed and she knows it."

"They're all doomed, all the Doops," Leo said. "And a good thing too. Who needs them?"

"*She* needs *herself*," Mina said. "She's all she's got. And she's different from the others: she knows it isn't enough."

"Well, thank you for making everything so clear," Leo said disgustedly. Then, "This orangeade is flat. I'll try the lime." He ripped the tab off a tin. "Ah, that's better," he said. He lifted the tin to the Doop guard. "Bung ho!" he jeered. "Cheers! Down the hatch!" He emptied the can and threw it at the Doop, as hard as he could.

The Doop picked up the can, inspected it solemnly

and handed it back to Leo. "Can for drink," he said.

"If you're trying to tell me," Leo said to Mina, "that the Princess is a precious little blossom filled with tender human yearnings – well, you're wasting your time. All I care about is getting *out* of here. *Escape*. You've got to help me. And if you're too busy to think of me, think of Boo. He's your little brother, remember?"

Mina, silent and furious, walked out of the hovel.

Leo shouted, "Come back!" after her. But she was gone. The guard did not try to stop her.

"You're a *guard*," Leo said. "Why don't you run after her and run her through with your nice rubber sword?"

The Doop looked earnestly at his sword, then answered, "Not allowed. Forbidden."

Leo arranged the cushions Mina had brought him. "Forbidden," he murmured. "Mustn't use your sword, right? Interesting."

He lay back on the cushions and made plans.

Pow

Escape, Leo thought. It shouldn't be difficult. The Doops were dopes. Their weapons were symbols, toys. For that matter, so were the Doops themselves; the "guards" didn't really guard, there were no splendid brains behind the splendid bodies. All show and no go. He could escape any time he wanted to.

But why escape? Escape to where? That was more difficult. He had to have somewhere to go to, someone to escape to.

For perhaps the thousandth time, he thought of his parents and fiddled with his radio – his only hope of contact with them. He scanned the frequencies. The radio made small, useless noises. It whooped, whined, beeped or imitated rushing water.

Then it said, so distinctly that Leo jumped, "PR37 02 Galax PR37 Clegg."

Leo began to shake. His fingers trembled so much that he could hardly operate the tiny controls. "Come on, come *on*!" he mumbled. "Once more! *Please*!"

"PR37," the radio said.

"Please, please!" Leo begged. "Clegg" was his surname; you never added your surname unless you yourself, a person with the surname Clegg, were the sender. A derelict ship manned only by dead humans might transmit, "PR37 02 Galax"; it would never add "Clegg".

" . . . 37 Clegg," the radio said, very faintly. Then the rushing-water noise took over.

Leo bent his head. Tears forced their way from his eyes and dripped on his arms. So faint, so faint . . . yet for a moment, he had *seen* his parents – seen his father rumpling his own hair and frowning, seen his mother tapping her teeth with a pen then, quick as a sparrow, leaning forward to make marks on a log sheet.

So faint, so faint . . . Yet as real and familiar as the smell that was, at this moment, tormenting him: the smell of an Earthside morning, the smell of coffee.

Coffee? *Coffee?*

Yes, definitely coffee. Unmistakable. What a pig Mina was! She'd found some real coffee and was no doubt enjoying it at this moment. None for brother Leo, of course. Let him rot in his kennel.

Not that it mattered. What mattered was the word "Clegg". He'd heard it, there was no doubt about it. It had come to him from somewhere out there to tell him that his parents lived.

Alive alive-O! He rubbed the tears out of his eyes and spoke loudly and clearly to his guard. "Grand day to be alive," he shouted, cheerily. The guard turned dead eyes on him.

"Lovely weather for the time of year!" Leo said.

The guard's stare was as leaden as the sky.

"Yes, it's good to be alive!"

The guard moved his lips uneasily.

"Well, it's been great having this little chat," Leo said. The guard said, "Uh?"

Leo lay on his cushions and resumed planning his escape. Escape was worth thinking about now. Somewhere out there, his parents lived and breathed. Somehow, they would reach him.

Mina, angry with Leo, went to the Princess. Together they tried on still more dresses – period costumes, garments of the nineteenth and twentieth centuries, ball gowns, fancy dress... the Princess's wardrobe seemed to go on for ever.

After half an hour of this, Mina became angry. The Princess never seemed to look properly at what Mina was wearing. She was interested only in herself. "I'm too young for black, aren't I?" she asked Mina. "Yes, I'm much too young. I mean, I'm all golden and gorgeous, black must be for old women with *white* skins."

"Do you like me in this?" Mina interrupted. She was trying on a sort of shepherdess costume with puffed sleeves, a nipped-in waist and a bouncy skirt. It really did go well with her fresh complexion, her springy, bronze-brown hair, her lively brown eyes. "I think it's just perfect for me," Mina said. "Don't you agree?"

Without looking at Mina, the Princess said, "Yes, definitely. I'm too young for black. Here, take it and put it away somewhere. And call me Your Majesty."

"Why certainly, Your Gracious – Imperial – *Majesty*!" Mina answered, glaring. The Princess did not notice the sarcasm or the glare. She just went on turning this way and that in front of the big gilt mirror, doting on her own reflection. Mina silently left. She would go back to Leo. She had been silly to quarrel with him. She'd make it up.

On her way to his kennel, she met Boo. He was riding on the shoulders of a Doop. He pulled the Doop's ears to guide him left or right. The Doop looked tired but made no complaint. Mina said, "I'm going to see Leo." Boo said, "I'm coming too. Gee up, Doop!"

When they reached Leo's hovel, the Doop fell down. He lay on the ground with his eyes wide open. The grille under his collarbone was wide open too. Boo said, "I wish they wouldn't do that." He bent over the Doop and waved his fingers in front of the Doop's eyes. "Wake up, Doop!" he cried. "Wake *up*! Be my horse!" The Doop's eyes and expression did not change.

Boo shook the Doop's shoulder. Mina looked on, fascinated. "Come on, get *up*!" Boo said. Then, "It's no good. I'll have to get another."

"You'll be lucky!" Leo called, from the doorway of his hovel. "Look around you!"

Mina and Boo looked. All the Doops they could see – a dozen or so – had slowed down or stopped. Some leaned against walls, some sat, some lay on the ground. There was nothing dramatic in their behaviour: their faces were placid.

And then the Warrior Queen appeared. "Cor," Leo whispered to Mina. "Look at that! Trendy new line in helmets! Get *her*!"

It was indeed a most gorgeous helmet: bronze and silver, with flame-like sweeping plumes of what might have been dyed ostrich feathers curling from it. She strode forward, holding a great spear in front of her. Four of her warriors walked in step with her, two on either side.

"New bits of armour, too," Leo said. "Very flash! Look at those shin-guards!"

The Warrior Queen halted by a fallen Doop. The haft of her spear rang as she struck the ground with it. "UP!" she ordered.

The Doop tried to obey. It made a slight movement, but could not rise.

"Link!" cried the Warrior Queen.

One of her guards bent down and grasped the hand of the fallen Doop. Its body twitched. Its eyes widened. It struggled to its feet.

"Link, link!" commanded the Queen.

Now all four of her warriors did as the first had done. As each Doop was revived, it joined hands with other Doops. Soon the Doops formed a semicircle, linked hand in hand.

"Now they play ring-a-ring-o-roses?" Leo murmured. He had freed himself from his bonds. His guard had long since joined the other Doops.

More and more Doops joined the semicircle. At last, the whole Doop population was linked. "Link, *link*, LINK!" they chanted.

"But where's the Princess?" Mina whispered to Leo. "Shouldn't she be here? Isn't she their ruler?"

Leo said, "Look! Now what?" The Warrior Queen was being lifted on to the shoulders of her guards. Her spear was handed to her. She straightened and stiffened her arm, thrusting the spear forward, pointing it

57

straight at the mountain.

"Pow!" she cried, her voice as firm and strong as her arm. "Pow!" the Doops shouted back. Their voices were ragged and uncertain.

"Charge!" cried the Warrior Queen. "Charge!" answered the Doops. Slowly, still hand in hand, they began walking towards the moutain.

"That's not *charging*," Boo said. "That's just *walking along*."

"Be quiet," Mina said. She was watching every move the Doops made.

"But charging's like *this*!" Boo foghorned. He made a ferocious face, leaned his body forward and made a series of charges. He gave up when he saw that Mina was not watching him.

The linked chain of Doops receded into the dull distance. Only the splendidly armoured Warrior Queen, perched high above the crowd, gave some sort of glamour to the procession.

"Fancy saying *Pow*," Boo complained. "Only babies say pow! Pow, pow, pow! What's *that* supposed to mean?"

"Let's find out," Leo said.

Leo, Mina and Boo followed the Doops towards the mountain.

When they were close to it, the mountain suddenly seemed bigger, more important, more imposing. Perhaps because it was the only high place on Argosy IV; more likely, because, close to, you became aware of the rich, coppery streaks that ran like rivers down its steep sides. But more likely still, because a feeling came from it, a feeling that did not belong to a mass of rock...

Boo was the first to notice it. "Is it *alive*?" he said.

"Don't be silly. Hills and mountains don't *live*, they just *are*," Mina told him.

Boo stared uncertainly at the mountain. "It could be alive," he said. "It's got veins." He meant the coppery streaks.

"They're not veins, they're just — just minerals, or ores, or something."

"It feels alive," Boo said. "It itches me."

Mina became aware that it "itched" her, too: ever since coming to the mountain she had been scratching her neck, rubbing her arms. She could think of nothing to say to Boo. So she concentrated on the Doops.

They were spread out. They were still holding hands. The grilles beneath their collarbones were wide open — so wide that she could have slipped her fingertips into them. She shuddered at the thought. The open grilles of the Doops nearest her seemed to pulse and strain. She had a sudden vision of tropical fish in tanks, and the way their mouths gaped open and shut...

The Warrior Queen stood high above the crowd, her erect figure glowing against the sullen rock of the mountain. She lifted her heavy spear and swung it like the vane of a weathercock above her head. It turned this way, the other way, slowly, slowly. The Doops' eyes followed its swing. "Pow!" they murmured. "Pow, pow!"

"*Pow!*" answered the Warrior Queen. Her wild hair made black waves around her shoulders as she turned her head, gazing into the eyes of one Doop, then another.

"Give me!" said a female Doop. She reached out her hands towards the Queen. Now she was no longer linked hand in hand, her strength left her. She fell to her knees. Her head bowed.

The Queen's lips drew back and her teeth flashed in a fierce grin. "Pow?" she shouted. "*Pow?*"

"She's teasing them," Boo said. "Mean."

"POW?" cried the Queen. Now her spear was swinging in a narrow arc, like the needle of a compass trying to settle.

"POW!" cried the Doops; and the spear straightened – quivered – and seemed almost to vibrate.

"Lined up with the mountain!" Leo whispered to Mina. "Look! Don't you see? That cave in the mountain – her spear's in line with it! Before she was just letting it swing about anywhere, but now it's —"

"It's going *all bright*!" Boo trumpeted.

And he might have been right. Certainly the gold of the spear seemed impossibly bright, almost luminous. But it quivered so much that you could not be sure.

"Ask!" cried the Warrior Queen. "Beg! Pray!"

The tip of the vibrating gold spear pointed above the heads of the Doops. Many of them reached above their heads and, with clutching hands, seemed to be trying to draw the tip down towards them. "Pow!" they cried. "Please pow!"

For a brief instant, the Warrior Queen dipped her spear. A dozen Doops at whom the tip pointed jerked, staggered, clawed at their grilles – and began a convulsive dance. From the rest of the Doops, voices shouted, "Pow!" Their upraised hands seemed to try to pull the spear in their direction.

"Beg!" shouted the Warrior Queen. The Doops begged. Some gabbled. Others tried to dance but fell. Still others howled, "Pow!" Give pow!" "Charge! *Please* charge!"

"Mean, mean! Teasing!" Boo bellowed. His little

60

face was screwed up with rage. They wanted pow – she had pow – why wouldn't she give them pow?

As if to answer him, she swung the spear slowly through an arc, its tip pointed at the Doops. The glowing – surely it was glowing? – and vibrating point picked out Doop after Doop; from the tip poured something invisible but real. Doops writhed, contorted, gabbled and danced. Some rubbed their arms with their hands.

"Why do they do that?" Mina was saying, when the tip of the spear swung to point straight at her and her brothers, and its force ripped into them.

There was a jolting shock, then a sudden warmth, then a prickling, fizzing itch. Nothing more. Yet on either side of them, Doops behaved as if caught in the blast of a bomb. Limbs writhed, faces contorted, legs jerked and flailed. Some Doops, when the dancing stage was over, rubbed themselves furiously. Again Mina began to ask, "Why do they —?" But the answer came before she could finish the question: pale blue fire, only just visible, seemed to flicker and crackle from the fingers of the rubbing hands. The fire wavered, waxed and waned – then somehow flung itself into the Doops' grille. "Pow!" cried the Doops when this happened. Then, "Pow, more!" cried the Doops, rubbing themselves still more furiously. But only sometimes did this produce more fire.

"I've got it!" Leo said. "Static electricity! Electricity of some sort, anyhow. And this is a sort of special ceremony —"

"This itching, it's driving me mad!" Mina said. "It's all over me!"

"Creepy-crawlies," Boo said. Like Mina he was picking at himself, scratching and rubbing.

"I can't stand it!" Mina said. "I'm getting out! Come on, Boo!"

"I want to stay and dance," Boo said. He began twitching and prancing. "Dance like the Doops," he said.

"Leo, are you coming with me?"

"No, not yet. It's electricity you see! She draws it from that cave in the mountain and then sprays it around. Her spear's a sort of lightning conductor. And we're watching the Big Recharge, the Let's-do-it-all-together ceremony! I want to watch. You go on, we'll follow."

Mina walked alone to the Princess's Palace. The itching died down.

"Your brother Leo is right," the Princess said to Mina. "Madra – the one you call the Warrior Queen – uses the spear to direct the power from the mountain into the bodies of the Doops. I'd have thought you would have known that. I thought you humans knew everything. You'd better put those dresses away, I've finished with them." Mina bit her lip and saw to the dresses.

The Princess said, "You must not call her 'Warrior Queen'. She is not a queen. Madra is just one of my servants. Simply a specially programed female Doop. *I* am the sole ruler here."

"Why did they keep saying 'Pow' to her?"

"'Pow' is their way of saying 'Power'. Like 'Charge'. They say that when they want to be *charged* with *power*. I'd have thought you'd have guessed that. Put the silver dress in the other wardrobe."

"Why do the Doops *dance*?"

"Address me as Your Majesty."

"Why do the Doops dance, Your Majesty? Why is the power-getting thing turned into a ceremony? Why can't the Doops simply open their grilles and get energy whenever they need it, on their own?"

"Oh, I like to keep an eye on my subjects. So I have this ceremony. I can see them and they can see me. But it got boring, so now I let Madra do everything. Of course, I keep an eye on Madra!"

"I see."

"Do be careful with that dress, the sequins come off. It's a Jazz Age dress. Do you know about the Jazz Age? Do you know when it was? I do. It was in the 1920s. Do you know about the Swinging Sixties? I do..."

Mina kept biting her lip and putting away dresses.

The smell of coffee...

Leo mentioned it. He greeted Mina with his usual bitterness, then said, "And while I've been mouldering away here, I suppose you've been pigging it in the Palace with Her Glorious Majesty. Stuffing yourself with roast swan and truffles."

"There aren't any swans on Argosy IV."

"If it weren't for Boo, I'd probably starve. While you pig away in the Palace."

"I eat the same food and drink the same drinks as you. Because it's the only food and drink there *is*. Supa doesn't eat or drink. Doops don't eat or drink. They exist on Pow, or Charge, or whatever you call it."

"*Do* they, now? So there's no special food for Her Majesty's favourites in the Palace? And no special drinks?"

"Look, how often do I have to tell you —"

"No special *drinks*? You're sure about that?"

"For the last time, Leo —"

"I mean, you haven't been drinking coffee recently, have you? Steaming cups of delicious coffee, while your brother drinks ten-year-old tins of fruit juice?" He rolled his eyes and made a martyred face.

Mina noticed, but she was thinking hard about more important things. "I haven't," she said, "been drinking *coffee*. Nor tea. Nor malted milk, or tiger's pee, or pearls melted in wine. So shut up."

"Well, all I can say," Leo said, "is that *someone*'s been drinking coffee."

Mina stopped thinking; she had come to a conclusion. Yes, someone had been drinking coffee; she didn't know who; and even if she did know, she wouldn't tell Leo.

Nor would she tell him about the big chimney or funnel or whatever it was, where the smell of coffee seemed to come from. She wouldn't tell him because (1) he was behaving like a pig; (2) because he was in no position to help — in fact, if he escaped and joined her in the search for the source of the Coffee Smell, he would give the game away simply by being absent from his hovel; and (3) because she wanted to do it all by herself.

The last reason was, though she would not admit it, the most important. She was tired of being bossed about by Supa. Tired of feeling guilty about enjoying trying on dresses when she should have been holding Leo's hand.

She rose to her feet and told Leo, "I'm sick of your moaning and fuss about coffee and I'm leaving you to stew in your own juice and *goodbye*."

She strode off feeling guiltier than ever.

Super-Super

She repeated her dawn walk the very next day, creeping out of the Princess's bedroom suite on all fours and holding her breath as she crawled past the sleeping Boo.

She could not avoid the Doop guards; but she was prepared to deal with them. She held out the Queen's whipping sash and said, "By special order of Her Majesty the Princess, I command you to let me pass!" She enjoyed saying these splendid words and was disappointed by the reaction of the guards; they merely looked vague and said "Uh?" as she pushed aside their blunt spearheads.

She made her way to the chimney, picking up pieces of rock as she walked.

She reached the rim of the chimney and felt her heart pound. She leaned over the rim. When she had done this before, the Princess had interrupted her. This time, the Princess was nowhere to be seen. Mina could concentrate.

Big, wide, rim; dark tunnel or shaft leading straight down. The grille. Darkness below. Nothing exciting to see, hear, feel or smell. Certainly no aroma of coffee.

Then her hair moved. Curls brushed her cheek and forehead. Her hair was lifting.

Good heavens! Mina thought, I'm so terrified that my hair's standing on end! She raised her head, surprised. Then she thought, But I'm *not* terrified. Not in the least! So what *is* happening?

Soon, it became obvious. There was a low, soothing whirr from the shaft. So a big fan had started up and her hair was being lifted by a current of warm air.

"Right!" Mina said aloud. She dropped a rock down the shaft.

Nothing happened. There was a dull sound – ploomp – as the rock landed on something, probably the grille.

She dropped another rock, then another.

The third stone struck lucky. There was an instant, appalling, deafening reaction from the shaft. "G–DANG!" it bellowed. "G–DANG! – RANG–A–BANG! – TACKER – TACK! – G–DANG, DANG, DANG!" Then *ploomp*, the soft sound as – so Mina guessed – the piece of rock bounced up from the fan blades and hit whatever protected them. The grille, almost certainly.

Then a voice from behind her.

"Really!" it said, in a peevish drawl. "Do you *mind*? I mean, *honestly!*"

Scarlet-nailed hands gripped Mina's arms. There

66

was a sudden small pain, a pinprick; then a tingling. She was pulled, protesting at first, across the broken ground. Her legs would not behave properly, they dragged and stumbled. She dreamed of walking in a tunnel, walking in darkness, stumbling, falling, getting up again ("Oh, do come *on!*") – and at last the walk was over, her head was ciearing and another voice was talking to her.

"Good, good!" it said. "So charming a child! But bad, bad, also. This is something we do not need, I think?"

It was a tall, fat, pale, dumpling of a man, a blond bladder. "Bleddy nuisance, yes?" he said.

"Absolute *pain*," said the first voice. "Blistering little *nuisance*. Still, it had to happen some time." The voice of a woman. An extraordinary woman wearing extraordinary clothes – swatches and slashes of dark and bright materials criss-crossing each other, held together with jangling chunks of arty jewellery.

The woman gripped Mina's hair in her long-nailed hand, and jerked Mina's head backwards so that she had to look up into the dead-white face haloed with lacquered spikes of black hair. The woman's black eyes were even blacker than her hair.

"Something we *particularly* don't need," the woman drawled, giving Mina's head a jerk.

Mina refused to show pain. "I know you," she said.

"*Do* you, now?" the woman said. "How nice for you. Who am I? Do tell. Hansi, light me a cigarette."

"Schmoking is bad," the man answered. He lit a cigarette and handed it to the woman. She poked it into her glistening red mouth and let go of Mina's hair. Mina fell backwards. "Do tell," she repeated.

Mina said, "You're like that woman in the ads, the

Doop ads. Long ago." She was pleased with the steadiness of her own voice.

"Not all *that* long ago," the woman said. Mina was trying to get up. The woman stretched out a thin foot in a black slipper crusted with fake jewels and pushed the girl back on the floor. "Go on about me," she said.

Mina said, "You were in the ads. When Doops were the new thing. You had Doops all round you, bringing you things and combing your hair and everything."

"So there you are, Madrigal!" Hansi said. He smiled and his eyes disappeared in the folds of his cheeks. "Still remembered! Immortal already!"

"*Was* it you?" Mina said. She was not sure. The woman in the ads had been like a beautiful cat, smooth and silken and purring; while this woman was a stringy ragbag held together with cosmetics and junk jewellery.

"So you know me," Madrigal said, "and I know you. All about you. And your dreary brothers – they are your brothers, aren't they? – crashing about in that schnitty old ship, getting everything wrong." She wagged her head in mock sympathy and tapped out the ash from her cigarette so that it fell on Mina. "Poor you," she said.

"And poor you," Mina said. "I mean, you haven't *lasted* very well, have you?"

Madrigal spat out some words and came at Mina with long fingernails flashing. Hansi thrust his bulk between them.

Mina said, "And another thing – people stopped saying 'schnitty' *ages* ago."

Hansi said, "Now now! Let us be friends! Yes, friends! Mina is a naughty girl, but so charming, so pretty, yes? And Madrigal is a naughty lady, but take no notice, inside she is all schweetness and light, is that

68

not so? Of course it is. So, we are friends. Come and sit on my knee, pretty child."

"No thank you very much," Mina said. She was on her feet now. "*You* sit on his crummy knee," she told Madrigal.

But the woman had lost interest. Her back was turned. She scraped at a front tooth with a badly lacquered fingernail and said, "What do we do with her, Hansi?"

"You could offer her some coffee," Mina suggested, nastily.

"Ah, so! That was it, the smell of the coffee!" Hansi said. "That led you to us!" He rambled on, always smiling, about coffee and delicious aromas and air vents. Madrigal scraped her tooth. Mina looked around her.

There was not a lot to see. The underground room was painted white. Madrigal – it must have been she – had splashed brilliantly coloured painted designs on one wall, but had given up. There were worn Earth-style chairs and domestic gadgets, including a coffee machine. Two long benches were cluttered with computers, unwashed crockery, small workshop machines and complicated mechanisms, all tiny and intricate.

The most interesting objects were three dressmaker's dummies: old-fashioned ones, solidly made from papier mâché covered with fabric. The dummies had big and small holes cut in them all over the place. By the holes were various handwritten letters and numbers.

Mina had seen enough. "I'm going now," she announced. "Nice to have met you, and goodbye." She went to the door, grasped the handle and turned it. The handle was dead. The door did not open. Mina said, "Let me out."

"Why so hurried?" Hansi said, with a smile like half a dozen crushed doughnuts. "Sit! Be comfortable! Soon, coffee. But first we play a game. Questions and answers, you like that? Of course."

"Goodbye," Mina said flatly.

Hansi loomed over her. He put a big, warm, soft, heavy hand on Mina's shoulder. She found herself sitting. "Questions and answers," he said.

"I can't tell you anything you don't already know," Mina said. "I want to *go*."

"Your parents," Hansi said. "Where are they? Will they come to collect you if they are living still? Or more likely, they are dead?" He beamed at her, his head cocked to one side.

Mina felt and looked sick. Madrigal said, "*Honestly*, I mean *really*," and glared at Hansi. Mina blurted, "Let me go."

Hansi said, "What wrong did I say? People live, people die." He shrugged his shoulders, reached behind him and pressed a button. "Coffee for our little visitor," he said.

On one of the benches, a machine squawked and made hideous grating noises. The noises made Mina jump. Hansi roared with laughter and said, "Nussings to fear, nussings at all! A coffee-grinder, merely!" Mina cursed herself for showing fear.

Just as the machine finished grinding the coffee, the door opened and a Doop entered.

It was like no Doop Mina had ever seen. It was a slim, neatly built, golden-skinned male, dressed as a waiter or steward. It moved with a swiftness and ease that even the Princess might have envied. The subtly changing expressions of its eyes and mouth seemed to suggest

70

a dozen different things, all flattering and soothing and confidential.

"The coffee," the Doop murmured in a soothing, musical, don't-mind-me undertone. "Allow me to make and serve it."

Mina stared at the Doop, fascinated.

Madrigal glared at it and shouted, "Get *out*, you stupid oaf!"

Hansi rose to his feet like a balloon escaping its tether and bellowed, "OUT! OUT! OUT!"

Mina watched the Doop's face. It showed, in quick succession, controlled surprise – humility – apology – submission. "I heard the coffee-grinder, so I thought you'd wish me to —"

"OUT! OUT! OUT!" bellowed Hansi.

"I'm so sorry. I'll leave at once." It left.

"My turn to ask questions," Mina said. "Question number one: who or what was *that*?"

"That," said Hansi, "is something you were not supposed to see. Explanations, yes? Very well... Once upon a time," he said, waving a plump hand as if to say, "I am being joky", "there were some very clever people, who did a very clever thing. They made Doops, yes? Beautiful Doops, to welcome, to serve, to take care of you —"

"I know all that," Mina said. "It didn't work. Because it wasn't quite clever enough. Or perhaps too clever. And the Doops had to be got rid of. So they were sent here, out of the way."

"And then?" Hansi said, still playing the part of the jolly old storyteller. "What then, pretty one?"

"Then the same clever people decided they'd better get still cleverer. So they hid themselves away and made a super Doop, the Princess. A better-luck-next-time Doop. And then, I suppose, a super-super-Doop, that servant thing. Look, can I go now?"

Hansi said, "Good, good! So charming *and* so clever! But now let us go on with the story. We reach the Princess. Now what is she? Just an exercise, a project? A truly good model with no faults and imperfections?"

"The Princess is all right," Mina said. "But she's not perfect. You'll never get Doops perfect."

"Ah!" Hansi said. He leaned forward and put his hand on Mina's knee. Mina pushed the hand away. "Ah, how true! One can never reach perfection."

"Hansi," Madrigal said, "do shut up. Serve the coffee, do anything, but button your lip."

"What harm is there to talk?" Hansi said, spreading his hands. "We understand each other, do we not, little one? Of course we do. Now, attend... Suppose you get the product right – but still no one *wants* it, you cannot sell it – what do you do then?"

"Hansi!" Madrigal said, warningly.

Mina said, "You find another use for the product. I suppose. I don't care what you do."

"Right, right!" Hansi said, creasing his face into doughnuts. "You find another *use*. Now, dear little friend, I will tell you something. *I* invented Doops. Oh, there were many assistants of course, but I alone was the creator!"

"He really *believes* it!" Madrigal said, throwing up her arms and rolling her eyes. "Alone he did it! All on his schnitty little owny-powny!"

"Madrigal *styled* the Doops, of course," Hansi said. "Madrigal did much to program them, to design their memory-stores —"

"And presented them, don't let's forget," Madrigal

said. "TV, personal appearances, *endless* drudgery."

"Look, *I'll* make the coffee," Mina said. "Then I'll go. All right?"

"You'll go?" Hansi beamed. "Oh, come, now!"

"You're not going anywhere, sweetie," Madrigal said, flatly.

"Of course you will not leave us," Hansi said, smiling. "Not now, when we are already such friends!"

"Just you try and stop me!" Mina said.

"I will, I will indeed!" Madrigal said; and shoved Mina backwards into a chair.

Mina felt herself grow cold but she said, "Look — please — let me go."

"Coffee," Hansi beamed. His flabby, heavy hand pressed Mina's shoulder, locking her in the chair. "Let Hansi give his little friend coffee."

No less than six guards appeared before Leo in his hovel.

"You are commanded," said the leader. His spear had gold tassels on it.

"Commanded to what?" Leo said.

"Commanded to come."

"Come where? Why?"

"Come."

The guards escorted Leo to the Palace. Once inside the entrance doors, they seized him and began tearing at his clothes. "Lay off that!" Leo shouted. He tried to fight free. He might as well have struggled with an earthmover.

A Doop thrust a finger into Leo's standard-issue undersuit and pulled. The high-resist fabric ripped, tearing into Leo's shoulder, cutting flesh like a blunt knife. Blood spurted. The guards were suddenly still.

They stared at the blood. The leader touched it with his finger; he even smelled it. "Wet," he said, vaguely. The other guards went on stripping their captive, but let Leo show them how to undo his clothes.

"You're going to kill me, aren't you?" Leo said. He was resigned. Obviously the Princess had grown tired of the whippings. Now she wanted a nice, gaudy death to amuse her. "I'm going to die, aren't I?" Leo said.

The guards flinched from the word as if it were a blow. "That word is forbidden!" the leader said and put a cold, hard hand over Leo's mouth. Leo wriggled free. "Sorry! My mistake! But what *are* you doing to me? *Why*?"

"Princess wants you," said the leader.

At one moment, Leo was almost naked. The next moment, guards were dressing him: dressing him in a velvet tunic – in soft leather pantomime-prince top-boots – in a floppy hat with a great plume of feathers – in sashes, belts, ruffs, ornamental daggers...

They finished. The leader said, "OK?" and pointed to a tarnished mirror. Leo inspected himself in it. He looked so completely ridiculous that he wanted to laugh. "Who's a pretty boy, then?" he squawked in his parrot voice, as he adjusted his plumed hat to a more rakish angle.

The Doops looked on expressionlessly. "OK," said the leader and led him to the Princess's apartments.

She received him seated on a great throne. Her jewelled skirts were arranged in a swirling cascade that tumbled elegantly down steps. She wore a crown: it was far too big and gaudy. This apart, she looked utterly beautiful.

"Good," she said. "You're properly dressed for the

occasion."

"What occasion?" Leo mumbled.

"Don't be stupid," the Princess said, waggling the jewelled sceptre she held in her left hand (a gold and crystal orb was in her right). "I can't stand stupidity."

"Oh, I'm sorry, I'm sure!" Leo said, hotly. "After all, I'm only a boring lout, a stupid male —"

"But males *aren't* stupid," the Princess said, earnestly. "I thought they were useless things – you know, like drones in the beehive – but I've re-checked. Males are *essential*. I would have thought you'd have known that."

"Essential for *what*?" Leo said.

"Marriages and babies," said the Princess.

"I beg your pardon?" Leo said, faintly.

"We're getting married today," the Princess said, "and then the baby will come. Quite soon. Come closer. Put out your hand. There! We're married!"

Leo looked down at his hand. On his third finger there was an enormous ring, mounted with what looked like pearls, rubies and diamonds.

"That's all," the Princess said. "We're married. Now you can go."

And then he was by the great doors again, dazed, with Boo trotting beside him. "What were you doing in there?" Boo demanded.

"Getting married, apparently," Leo said.

"*Married*?" Boo foghorned. "Who *to*?"

"The Princess."

Boo thought about this and said, uncertainly, "She's pretty..."

"There's that," Leo said gloomily.

"I'd rather marry Ma, wouldn't you?" Boo said.

"Marry my mother," Leo said. "Yes, I suppose that makes sense too."

"Ma's not as pretty as the Princess," Boo said. "But she's nicer."

"Suppose *you* marry her," Leo suggested.

"Da wouldn't let me," Boo said. "You know Da."

He lost interest and started running in circles, making spaceport noises. His imitations were amazingly accurate. Leo looked on without seeing. "Not even a teenager, and married to a Princess," he said to himself. He stared in the mirror. A pantomime Prince Charming in a plumed hat stared back at him.

"Congratulations," he muttered, hollowly, to his reflection.

Not Permitted

From somewhere outside the room, a bell rang insistently. "Oh-oh," Madrigal said. "The timer. Back to work. Come on, Hansi."

Hansi rose to his feet like a soft balloon and followed Madrigal to the door. He turned and said, "Now I must leave my little girlfriend, yes? But soon I will return, do not fear."

"Don't hurry," Mina said, nastily.

"Don't you be cheeky," Madrigal said to Mina, glaring. Mina stared back, coolly. "You offered me coffee," she said. "That nice-smelling coffee, remember?"

Madrigal glared and lifted her hand. But the timer bell was still shrilling, the woman had to go. Hansi rolled his eyes at Mina and said, "Coffee, of *course*!

Anything your heart desires! I call Jeeves, the one you called super-super-Doop. So amusing."

Madrigal and Hansi left. Jeeves entered, "Yes, Miss?"

"Something to drink. Anything," Mina said.

"Did I hear you mention coffee, Miss?"

"Yes. No, wait..."

Mina was thinking hard. If I ask for coffee, Jeeves will serve it here, from that machine. But if I ask for something else, he'll have to leave me on my own while he goes to fetch it. Then I can have a good look round...

"Lime juice?" Mina said. "Or passion-fruit juice? Have you got those?" She was hoping he would have neither and would have to leave her on her own.

"Yes, Miss. Either. Both." Jeeves bowed but made no movement.

"Passion-fruit juice, then."

"Certainly, Miss." Still he did not move.

"Well, go and get it for me, please."

"Certainly, Miss, as soon as Master and Mistress return."

"No, *now*."

"I am instructed to keep you company, Miss."

"Well, I cancel the instruction. You can go."

"Oh, no, Miss! I must insist on keeping you company."

Mina thought, Well, that's that: they're several moves ahead of me. They guessed what's in my mind. And they can talk to Jeeves without talking. Now what?

"If you're going to spy on me," she said, "you might as well sit down and make yourself comfortable."

"I'm quite comfortable standing, Miss."

"Are you comfortable all the time, Jeeves? Do you never get tired?"

"Only when I – oh, no, Miss. Not ever."

"You started to say, 'Only when I'. Only when you *what*?"

"May I serve you with coffee, Miss?"

"Only when you *what*?"

"This is real coffee, Miss. The finest Blue Mountain from Earthside. Do you wish milk or cream? Most ladies like a little cream."

"When do you get tired, Jeeves? What makes you tired?"

Jeeves would not answer. He attended to the coffee machine. He poured ground coffee into a glass bowl.

Mina went to him and stood close to him. "You never get tired, never get impatient, never get anything wrong, Jeeves?"

"I try my best, Miss."

She prodded the glass bowl with a rigid forefinger. The bowl toppled. The ground coffee spread like sand.

Without a word, Jeeves swept up the coffee and refilled the glass bowl.

Mina knocked it over again.

After the fifth upset, Jeeves's hands moved jerkily as he swept up the spilled coffee.

"Call up the Master, Jeeves! Or the Mistress! They'll come to your rescue, won't they?"

"I am not permitted – I mean, I do not need – to interrupt them at work."

"You mean 'not permitted'. Interesting!" Mina said.

She picked up bowls containing lump and granulated sugar. She threw the lumps all over the floor. She poured the granulated sugar into the neck of Jeeves's tunic. He stood still while she did it, then beat at himself as if smothered with biting insects and said, "But – but – "

Now all his movements were jerky.

Mina ran round the room, tipping over chairs, sweeping papers and equipment off tables, creating havoc. "But – but...!" said Jeeves.

"But – but – but – but – but!" Mina echoed, like a motorboat. Over her shoulder, she observed every uneasy move the robot made. "Why don't you *tell* them!" she jeered. "Why don't you *call* them?"

"It is not – not permitted – when at work..."

"Work at *what*?" Mina said, knocking down a table lamp. Clumsily, Jeeves picked it up and tried to replace it on the table. The lamp fell through his fingers and smashed on the floor. "I will serve coffee, coffee..." he said. His eyes were rolling. "*What* work?" Mina insisted. "Coffee..." Jeeves said; and collapsed.

Mina stood over his fallen body. "So you never get tired, right?" she said. "Never need charging? Never need pow?"

Jeeves said, "Pow... Pow..."

Mina said, "Jeeves, tell me, what are Master and Mistress doing? What work?"

Jeeves said, "Pow. Please. Then serve coffee Blue Mountain."

Mina said, "I will break more things if you don't talk sense."

"No, please! No more. Is tired. Needs pow."

"All right, Jeeves. You are tired, you must have pow. Come with me, I'll give you pow."

She was wondering why Madrigal and Hansi could not give their servant a charge whenever he needed it; after all, it was only static electricity or something like that. She asked Jeeves. He said, "Busy other things. No time for Jeeves's pow. Is tired, give pow." Even his voice was breaking down.

"Come on then," she said. "Outside. Come on, you can do it."

Mina saw that he had a plastic thing on his jacket, a little tab on a watch chain. It opened doors that swung, doors that slid. They climbed stairs until above them, dull light glimmered.

Then they were in the open and Jeeves was draped over the mouth of the ventilator shaft, his eyes flickering, knees buckling, fingers twitching. "Pow," he gasped. "Help me to pow."

The plastic tab swung from its chain. Mina took it and jerked: the chain snapped. "Not permitted!" Jeeves protested. "Please... Give back."

"But you want pow, don't you?" Mina said.

"Yes, pow. Please give pow."

"It's over there," Mina said nodding her head at the mountain. "Straight on, you can't miss it. Bye-bye."

She strode away, swinging the tab on its chain. "Pow! Pow!" Jeeves called after her. Even his voice was failing.

She walked on, not turning her head.

Mina went to the Princess's apartments. The Princess might tell her about the work being done by Hansi and Madrigal. She knocked on the door of the Princess's apartment. "You may enter," cried the sweet, childish voice.

"There's something I must know," Mina said. "*Please*, Your Majesty – tell me what is happening."

Before she could finish, the Princess said, "Oh, but you must know! Everyone knows! An historic occasion!"

"Your Majesty, listen to me —"

"An historic occasion," the Princess said. "A royal marriage! Why weren't you there? I would have permitted you to be present! How selfish and thoughtless you are. I am very angry with you for missing it! Truly angry! I shall have him whipped for it!"

"But Your Majesty —"

"No, I can't have him whipped any more, can I? Not now he is my husband, royal like myself! Not now the baby is on the way. First the lovely wedding, then the lovely baby! Oh, Mina, Mina, I am so happy!"

Mina, stopped in her tracks, said, "What do you mean? What marriage? What baby?"

"Prince Leo, of course! I thought you would have known. After all, he is your brother! But now he's my husband, too. No, that's wrong, you are my sister-law and the baby is your daughter-law... No, wait..."

As the Princess scanned her memory units, Mina stared dumbly at the perfect face – at the little frown of concentration between eyebrows like delicate brush-strokes – at waves and tendrils of golden hair – at the lovely curves of chin and cheek...

Mina stared; and once again was swept by a feeling of tenderness and compassion for the beautiful toy, the mechanical fantasy, the lost soul without a soul.

"Sister-in-law!" the Princess cried, as a memory clicked into place. "Isn't that exciting? We'll be almost sisters! But best of all, the baby! My baby! It's coming very soon, did I tell you? Because I am now a married woman. It will be *mine*... *of* me, *from* me! And so I won't just finish – come to an end – I won't *die*, part of me will live! Through my baby!"

Mina took the Princess's perfect hand and held it.

"There, you see!" the Princess cried. "I said the forbidden word – 'die' – and it didn't affect me at all! Die, death, dead... They're only words, aren't they? Weak words."

"Only words," Mina said, pressing the perfect hand.

"Are you happy for me?" the Princess said. "*I* am! Because everything will be so lovely!" She sprang to her feet. "Look, I already have my clothes ready for when the baby comes! All my prettiest things! Do you like this little crown? Do the stones match my eyes? I think they do. And this skirt..."

Mina's heart and brain cooled. The Doops, Jeeves, the Princess... They were all the same thing: merely *things*. And yet...

She looked out of a window and saw Boo. He was "flying", with his arms outstretched and his mouth making brrr–brrr–vroom flying noises. He was human and real. What was the Princess compared with him? Nothing. Boo came first. Boo, Leo and Mina.

"Your Majesty," Mina said. "Please tell me something. It's very important to me."

"Anything!" said the Princess. "Do you like these slippers? I'm not sure I do. But never mind, ask your question."

"Look out of the window. Did you know there are people – humans – living under there?"

"Where? Oh, over there. Under the vent. Yes. Two of them. No, I am wrong. I don't know what you are talking about, *nobody* lives there. Nobody at all."

"Please, Supa! You *do* know what I'm talking about. You said 'two of them'. You know there are two humans."

"There's nobody there. Nobody at all."

"Two of them, Supa."

83

"How dare you contradict me! I shall have him whipped! Yes, I shall! Beat your brother! The little one, I mean, not Leo. He is my prince. The little one is my new whipping boy."

"Two of them, Your Majesty. From Earthside. Why are they there? Have you met them? Have they spoken to you? What are they doing?"

"I shall wear this white lace shawl when the baby comes. Mothers wear shawls. And the little crown, of course."

"The woman is called Madrigal. The man is called Hansi."

The Princess swung round, eyes blazing – and slapped Mina's face. "Don't dare mention those names to me!" The Princess stormed. "That Madrigal – she is a *beastly, a vile*, a – a *filth*!" With each word, she aimed another wild slap. Mina easily dodged them.

"Why, Supa? Why is she so bad?"

"She did things to me," the Princess whispered, her rage suddenly gone. "She made me do things."

"What things?"

"She called them Tests. They were numbered. There were many numbers adding up to a Series, or something. They kept putting different things in my head."

"They? Hansi did it too?"

"Oh, Hansi is nice. He was always so sorry when the test hurt. So kind. Always smiling."

"I can imagine," Mina said, drily.

"They *adjusted* me," the Princess said. "That was it. Fine Adjustments and Tests. My brain, my memory units, everything. She didn't mind how much it hurt..."

"Poor Supa."

"You should call me, Your Majesty," the Princess

84

said, vaguely. "Once, they took out my eyes when my sensors were still live. I can't tell you... Have you ever had your eyes pulled out?"

"No."

"Don't let them do it to you, not ever. And they shortened my spine, it was horrible."

"What are they after, Your Majesty? What do they want?"

"They wanted me perfect. And I am."

"But what *else* do they want?"

"I don't know. *They* don't know. It's the Galaxy, something to do with the Galaxy."

"The Galaxy? I don't understand."

"They want to *rule* it, or something. They're making things to *rule* it. Aren't they stupid? *I* am the Princess. I rule over everything."

"Of course you do, Supa. But... Rule the Galaxy? How could they rule anything from that hole in the ground?"

"What hole in the ground?"

"Where Hansi and Madrigal live. Over there. That funnel or vent or whatever."

"There is nobody there," the Princess said primly. It was as if a switch had clicked inside her. "Nothing, nobody. Not ever. Now go away. No, wait. These slippers: are they right for the mother of a baby?"

Mina went straight to Leo. He had to be told everything. "Leo, are you there? Wow! You do look a fool dressed like that!"

Leo threw his feathered hat at her and said, "Tell me something new."

"Yes, that's why I'm here. To tell you things. Listen..."

At first, he did not want to hear. "You've been dreaming," he said. But when she showed him the tab that gave entrance to the underground stronghold, his expression changed. "You mean, this lets us into the place?"

"Yes. But only *now*, not later. Later they're bound to find Jeeves missing. Or they'll find *me* missing."

"And right now, they're getting on with their work?" Leo said. "Preparing to take over the Galaxy and all that. That's what you think they're doing?"

"They plan to rule the Galaxy," Mina said, patiently. "It's no good pulling that face. They mean it. Rule Earth and all the other worlds we know about in the Galaxy."

Boo said, "That's silly. We've got rulers already. Rulers for Earth and everywhere. The Fed–er–a–tion. I know from school."

Leo said, "You must admit, Mina, Boo is probably right. I mean, two loonies in a dugout couldn't invade Earth, let alone the whole Galaxy."

Mina said, wearily, "Look, I don't *know* what anybody can or can't do. I only know what I was *told*. And I think we've got to *do* something. Find out more, at any rate. As soon as possible."

Boo said, "I'm coming. I want to see."

Mina said, "Look, Boo! There's your horse waiting for you!" She pointed to an aimless-looking Doop.

"Don't want to ride. Want to go with you."

But Leo had already picked him up, hoisted him on the shoulders of the Doop and told Boo, "Grab his ears, Boo! Off you go!"

Off he went.

"Let's get going," Mina said.

They made their way to the chimney.

Boo waited till his horse-Doop had carried him well away from Mina and Leo; then said, "Horse, stop. Put me down." Now Boo was alone.

"My da," he muttered. He trotted back to the Palace, keeping a sharp look-out for Leo and Mina. He did not want to be seen. He was on a Secret Mission.

At the great doors, Doop guards tried to bar his entrance. Boo scowled and pushed their spears aside. "Don't 'trupt me," he foghorned. "Don't want no 'truptions. Want my da."

Inside the Palace, he looked about him and almost at once found what he was looking for: a heap of clothes. Leo's clothes. He sorted through the pile, flinging aside the garments. Then he said, "Ah!" and smiled.

Leo's watch. The watch with the radio in it. It was still going.

He took it and ran off to a quiet and hidden place. He began prodding the watch's little buttons. "Da?" he said. "Da? It's me. It's Boo. Da? Are you there, Da?"

For a long, long time, nothing happened. But Boo was both clever and determined. He kept prodding the watch's buttons. At last the watch spoke.

"02 Galax PR37 Clegg," it said.

"Da! I'm Boo! Don't go. I'm Boo!"

"PR37 Galax PR37 Clegg."

"Talk properly, say proper things! It's me, it's Boo!"

"PR37 Galax – Oh Boo, darling Boo! Oh, precious lovely darling baby!"

"Ma, is that you? Ma, it's not a baby, it's Boo."

"Darling, darling, Boo..."

"They're 'vading," Boo said. "Bad people. Loonies. Going to 'vade. Da has got to stop them. Where is Da?"

"Boo, I can't hear you, you keep fading…"

"'VADING!" Boo foghorned.

"Boo, my darling! You're all right? And Mina and Leo? Tell me you're all right!"

"*I'm* all right. And *Mina's* all right. And *Leo's* all right, but he's a prince. He's got a hat with feathers."

"Darling Boo… You're alive and well? Are you?"

"I keep *telling* you. We're ALL RIGHT. Ma, I miss you. You and Da. Why don't you come before they 'vade? Ma, you've got to *come*, I *want* you."

"Boo, I can't hear you. Can you hear me? I think you can. Say you can. Say, 'Yes, I hear.'"

"Yes, I hear."

"Then listen, Boo! Listen, and tell Leo and Mina. Tell them a Paxforce ship is on its way to you, do you understand that? A Galax Paxforce ship. It's on its way. Did you hear?"

"Yes, I heard. But hurry, because they're 'vading. And I WANT you. You and Da!"

All at once, everything went wrong. The voice of the radio became whistles and screeches and howls, or echoing blankness; and Boo found himself in tears, crying so loudly that even if a signal had managed to break through the noise, he would not have heard it.

Underground

The tab that had got Mina out of the underground hideaway gave them their way in. It was easy. "Too easy," Leo said nervously.

"Oh, come *on*," Mina replied, leading him down the long, sloping corridor connecting the underground apartments to the world outside. The corridor was featureless, dimly lit, rough-hewn and the shape of a D lying on its flat side. "Done with a laser cutter," Leo commented. He paused to examine the characteristic marks underfoot, like the coarse grooves of antique gramophone records. "Come *on*," Mina said. She was very nervous. It was all right for Leo: he had never met Madrigal and Hansi. She had. "Don't lag," she said.

Then she stopped dead. Ahead of her lay something

she had not expected: the corridor fanned out into three separate tunnels.

"Well?" Leo said. "Which is ours?"

Mina stared at the three identical openings. At last, she said, "I don't... *know*!"

"But you must know! You've been here before!"

"I tell you, I *don't*. I was in a panic. I just went on and on. I came out of *one* of these tunnels, but I don't know which..."

"But you *must*..." Leo began; and stopped. Behind them following them down the tunnel, there was the sound of footsteps. Deliberate, unhurried footsteps, coming closer.

"Oh, no! Please no!" Mina said.

"Mina – which *way*?" Leo hissed in her ear.

"I don't *know*, I just don't know!"

The footsteps echoed louder and nearer.

"Come on, then!" Leo said. He seized her wrist and jerked her forward into the tunnel on the right. "This one's as good as any," he muttered.

Mina was sobbing. She had been brave for too long in front of Hansi and Madrigal. Now her bravery was all used up.

"Now what?" Leo said.

The way ahead was blocked by a strong door taken from an Earth-style cargo ship.

"Tab!" Mina said wildly. In the gloom, between sobs, she pushed the tab at the door hoping that somewhere there would be a slot.

There was no slot.

"Those footsteps!" Leo said. They were very close now. Mina sobbed. "Slot...! Please, let there be a slot!" Leo jerked his head from side to side looking for a place to hide. The footsteps were very close. "Come on!" he whispered, grabbing her arm. "Here!" He pulled her into a shaded recess. "Don't cry!" he grated in her ear. She stifled her sobs.

And then the footsteps were *there*, right on top of them – and they could make out the figure that caused them: the disciplined, upright figure of Jeeves. Jeeves looked neither to the right nor the left. He extended a neat hand, grasped a small, recessed handle – turned it – opened the door – and was gone.

Mina was free to cry again. She sobbed. Leo wanted to laugh. It was too ridiculous! – all you needed to do was turn the door handle! For half a minute he laughed and she cried. Then Mina said, "I'm all right now. What do we do?"

"We go on. Look inside. What else are we here for?"

"OK. Follow me." She gritted her teeth and, very quietly, opened the door and stuck her head through the gap. Satisfied that neither Jeeves nor anyone else was there, she said, "Come on."

Now it was Mina's turn to laugh. "Guess what!" she said. "We've found the servants' entrance!" They were in a small kitchen, spotlessly clean, brightly lit and excellently equipped. "Dinner for two, please, Jeeves!" she giggled. Leo said, "Be *quiet*, he might hear you."

"I was expecting a robot army," she whispered, "not a robot *cooker*!"

"Shut up. Come on. Jeeves is back, remember. He's bound to have spilled the beans to Hansi and what's-her-name."

"Beans...!" Mina said, and started giggling again.

They left the kitchen and found a room full of wines in racks; a room with various sorts of clothing in it, including some space gear with dim-looking glassine helmets – "Not been used for years," Leo murmured; big rooms containing chemical and engineering supplies of every kind; and then a corridor with doors leading out of it. The sight of the doors silenced both of them. Anyone and anything could be on the other side of the doors.

They stood still for some time, just listening. No voices, no lights. At last Leo whispered, "This one, OK?" Mina nodded.

The door had a slot for the tab, also a handle. Mina said, "Try the handle first, less noise." The handle was dead. She shrugged and inserted the tab. The faint whirring she was afraid of took place, but not too loudly. The door was open.

It led into an enormous room, endlessly long.

The room was stacked, from floor to ceiling, with bodies.

Small lights cast a chill radiance over the ranks and banks of close-packed forms. It was as if the bodies had been drilled: "Right – close up tight – tighter than that! Now *die*." And all the bodies had obediently dropped identically dead, feet angled identically, chins and noses jutting identically into the cold light.

Mina started shivering. "Cold... so cold," she muttered. Leo said, "Well, what do you expect? Morgues are always cold, they've got to be..." He wanted to sound gruff but his voice was high and croaking. "Going to have a proper look," he said; and made himself inspect the nearest of the bodies. Mina turned her head away and tightly closed her eyes. Each body was covered, from neck to ankle, with a thin, milky, semi-transparent plastic sheet. Leo gritted his teeth and ripped a sheet away. What he saw made his jaw drop and his eyes widen.

"Mina! Have a look! A good look! Come on, there's nothing to be afraid of."

She forced her eyes open and looked. Her eyes, too, widened. "*No toes,*" she gasped. "Feet without toes!"

"And hardly any fingers," Leo said. He lifted a lifeless, cold, smooth hand. The hand was more or less human, but horribly simplified. "Thumb, first finger," Leo said. "The other fingers are just welded together." He made himself squeeze the dead flesh, feeling for bones. "No bones after the thumb and first finger," he said. "Just a flexible plate." He was proud of talking so calmly, without a quaver. But holding the hand made him feel sick.

Mina was brave again. She walked along a line of bodies, pulling away the plastic sheets. "All exactly the same," she said. "Identical. And no nostrils, no navels, no genitals, no hair, no nails. And no teeth in the mouths. I wonder why they need mouths?"

"Like another hand," Leo said. "Something to hold things with. To operate things. Tools, things like that."

"Not tools: weapons," Mina said. "What else?"

They sat down. "Seen one, you've seen 'em all," Leo said. Around, above and beyond them lay rack upon rack of silent, motionless bodies. At last, Leo said, "So this is it: the invading army. The new rulers of the Galaxy."

"I don't believe it," Mina said. "These things are no good. They can't think, they've no will..."

"What were the names of your friends?" Leo said. "Hansi and the other one?"

"Hansi and Madrigal."

"Well, *they* can think. And *they've* got wills."

"All the same..." Mina began, but could not finish.

93

She stared at the endless lines of bodies. "I hate them," she said, very quietly.

"Oh, I don't know!" Leo said. "You'll find them the best of pals once they've taken over. I mean, *they* don't hate *you*. When they exterminate you and throw your body into the big pit, there'll be no ill-feeling. Just zap-zap-zap, nothing personal, you're dead, on to the next one."

Mina just bit her lip and stared at nothing. At last, she said, "We must be mad, just sitting here! We've got to do something!"

A voice answered her. "Oh, no, please!" it said. "You must stay! For we are old friends already, yes? Yes! You are my pretty little schweetheart, isn't that so? And now brother Leo is here too. So nice!"

Hansi's voice.

Paxforce

The Commander of the Paxforce ship said, "Galax PR37 Clegg, you reading?"

"Reading. Tom Clegg speaking."

"OK, fine. What do you want us to do? Collect you and your wife first, then go on to Argosy IV; or go straight away to Argosy to rescue your kids?"

"Hold on a minute. I've got to talk to my wife."

The Commander overheard the mumble of voices. He rattled his fingernails impatiently on the table for some seconds, then cut through the mumble. "Look, I need a decision *now*. I mean, I *can* pick you up – we're only minutes apart – but there's the locking and docking procedure when our two ships come together. And frankly, that ship of yours —"

"Tom Clegg speaking. Look, there's nothing wrong with our ship! Everything's operational. Well, almost."

The Commander heard a woman's voice say, "Tom, let them go in straight away! Boo said something's *happening* on Argosy —"

Then he heard Clegg's voice saying, "But I want to *be* there, Ellie. I want to be the first to —"

Once again, the Commander cut through. "*Do* I go straight in without you, or do I waste time picking you up? It's your decision. Please make it."

A long pause, then Clegg's voice told the Commander, "You go in. We'll follow you just as soon as I've fixed the Navigator Mode. It's almost done, I've just got to —"

"Thank you. Now proceeding Argosy IV. Out."

The radio went dead. Tom and Ellie Clegg stared at each other, silently. "I just wish we could be the first to see them, hold them," Tom began. But then their ship seemed to flinch and rock as, not far away, the Paxforce ship's drives belched shock-waves.

"Well, that's that," Ellie said. "They're off!"

Tom Clegg had been bending over the Navigator Mode console. Now he straightened up. He was smiling. "I don't believe it!" he grinned. "Look! I've got readouts! And they're making sense!"

Ellie answered by fanning her fingers over the Drive console. Lights twinkled. The ship's drives hummed, whined, howled, screeched. The screeches settled down into a roar. "On our way!" she said. "We'll arrive late – but we'll be there!"

The drives roared. The old ship bashed on. The Navigator Mode pointed firmly to Argosy IV.

Ellie and Tom hugged each other.

*　　　　　*　　　　　*

Hansi's voice had come from a viddyspeak on the wall. The speak's eye stared dully at Mina and Leo. Then Hansi himself stood in the doorway, his eyes glimmering fondly in his puffy face. "Your pretty sister and I, already we are such good friends!" he said. He made as if to stroke Mina's hair. She drew back. Hansi stretched out his hand for Leo to shake. Leo ignored it.

"So, so!" Hansi beamed. "Now you will come with me, to meet Madrigal." He led the way. Jeeves, who had appeared from nowhere, followed behind. But first he said to Mina, "My tab, if you please." She handed it to him.

They came to the room Mina already knew. Madrigal stood with her back turned to them. Four cups were laid out on the table. Coffee had already been prepared. Jeeves poured it. "Oh, yes, we were expecting you," Hansi said, smiling with his head cocked to one side. "We watched you come in, yes? The kitchen first, and then —"

"Oh, shut up, Hansi," Madrigal said, swinging round and flinging panels of her dress behind her. She was in a rage. "Give the little morons their coffee and then... No, give me a cigarette first, light it for me."

Hansi obeyed. "Schmoking is not good for you," he said, wagging his great smiling face tenderly. "How many times I am telling you?" Jeeves handed round coffee. Mina and Leo scowled as they took their cups. But the coffee was so delicious that it softened the mind. With such soft cushions to lean back on, with such almost-forgotten tastes and smells, surely there could be nothing to worry about, ever again?

"I don't know what the hell to do with you two," Madrigal burst out. She marched up and down, dress swirling, jewels clanking and flashing. "Obviously you've got to be got *rid* of, *disposed* of, but *how*? Hansi, suggest something sensible for once!"

"Yes, to be got rid of," Hansi sighed. Before Mina could stop him, he had taken her hand in his great, soft paw and was patting it. "Such a shame!" he crooned. "To lose my dear little girlfriend, even before we..." She pulled her hand away. He sighed and said to Madrigal, "You are right, dear Madrigal. They must go. Go they must. But not in such a way as to cause suspicion. The Federation, the Inspectorate, the Paxforce... They must not see anything suspicious. Difficult, so difficult." He wagged his head and looked as if he might burst into tears.

"Then there's the third one, that hideous little ape of a baby brother," Madrigal said, stubbing her cigarette into her coffee. "He's got to go too. *Three* Earthside-registered bodies to dispose of! *Three*, Hansi! Of course, it will end up with *me* doing it, it's always *me*. I'm sick and tired of... Jeeves, this smells filthy, *do* something." She held out her coffee cup to the Doop. He silently made off with it, quietly closing the door behind him.

Mina thought, That leaves the two of them. She got to her feet.

Madrigal said, "Hansi, a cigarette. Light it for me." Again, the tender shake of the massive head; again, the fat fingers and fat lips nursing a cigarette, lighting it, handing it over...

Mina caught Leo's eye. He followed her rapid meaningful glances flickering from lighted cigarette to coffee cup. He got to his feet.

"More coffee?" he said, and filled his cup to the brim. The coffee machine kept the coffee very hot.

Madrigal took furious puffs from her cigarette, blew

smoke, swirled her amazing dress and strode up and down.

"We could *age* them," she said to Hansi. "Had you thought of that? Of course not, I have to think of everything. We could stick the bodies in the dissimulator, just as we used to do with Doops to harden up the skin. I mean, a really good dissing would *age* the tissues, wouldn't it? Then we'd pop them in the freezer. Then we'd be able to say the kids were dead on arrival."

Madrigal, her waving arms outstretched, walked past Mina. Mina snatched the burning cigarette from the taloned fingers.

Hansi, seated, his chins bulging over the hand on which they rested, was listening earnestly to Madrigal. Leo stood before him, offering a cup of hot coffee.

Mina threw the lighted cigarette down the back of Madrigal's dress.

Leo flung the hot coffee into Hansi's face.

Suddenly the room was a zoo at feeding time – high-pitched screechings, hoarse bellowings and trumpetings, frantic and meaningless rushings to and fro.

"Time to go," Leo said, courteously.

"After you," Mina replied, politely.

They ran.

Somehow, they found their way to the kitchen; and Jeeves. He had become a clockwork toy, completely lost in the welter of sounds – the bellowings of Hansi, the screechings of Madrigal – pouring from the little loudspeaker in the wall. Jeeves was programed to obey the speaker when it said, "Come here, make coffee," or "Bring lunch," or "Come and clear up,"; but *these* sounds! – these yells and shrieks! He could make nothing of them.

"Put me out, put me OUT!" screamed the voice of Madrigal. Jeeves gaped vacantly.

Mina nudged Leo's arm and said to Jeeves, "Go on, then! Obey your mistress! Do what she says!"

Jeeves said, "Certainly. Right away. Not at all. As you wish. Yes."

Leo said, "Can't you hear her? She's saying, 'Put me out!' So you've got to put me out, like she says!"

"Me too!" Mina said. "You must 'put me out' too! Immediately!"

"Immediately," Jeeves echoed. "Certainly. Forbidden. Not at all. Allow me. Lightly chilled. I beg your pardon."

Leo and Mina stood on either side of Jeeves, shouting in his ears. "Out, *out*, OUT!" they bellowed. They pushed against him. He swayed, stumbled, bowed from the waist, jerkily rubbed his neat little hands...

Then led them through the underground tunnel to freedom.

"Keep walking!" Leo told Mina. She had wanted to rest – to lean her forehead against the coolness of the rim of the vent – but Leo wouldn't let her. "Boo," he said. "Got to get to him before *they* do. Or Jeeves does."

"Jeeves won't do anything," Mina said. "Look at him!"

Jeeves was still in his clockwork-toy condition. He stood at the exit from the underground stronghold and walked stiffly in little circles. "Certainly," he said. "Yes. No. On a tray or laid out on the table? At once. Allow me."

100

"Don't have to worry about him," Leo said. "Let's concentrate on finding Boo."

As he spoke, a foghorn voice said, "Going to rain!" and Boo was there beside them. He allowed Mina to hug him for several seconds; then pushed her away firmly. "Better get indoors," he said. "Going to rain."

"What do you mean, Boo? The sky's not dark, or anything."

"Well, thunder, then. Big thunder – barrroom, *whoompf*."

"Don't be silly —"

"*Listen*," Boo ordered, turning his face to the sky. Leo and Mina listened. "That's strange," Leo said to Mina. "Can you hear it?"

"I don't hear anything. No, wait..."

Now even the nearby Doops heard something. They lifted their heads to the dull sky and stood still, listening to the distant, thunderous throb.

"Told you so," Boo said. "Thunder."

"Not thunder," Leo said. "More like... more like..."

"A spaceport, when a ship's expected!" Mina said. "You know what I mean. The ship's hundreds, thousands, of miles away, but it stirs up the atmosphere, you get that booming noise."

"Spaceport," Boo said. "Oh, yes." He gave his excellent spaceport imitation.

But then the distant throb was flooded by other sounds: sounds from the stronghold's vent. First a rising whine that steadied into a continuous, powerful hum; then a grumbling roar that filled your head.

"What's it all *about*, what does it *mean*?" said Mina. The Doops seemed to know. They crowded in fast, heading for the rim of the vent. "Their slots are open,"

Leo said. "Wide open! Perhaps they sense pow coming out of the vent."

"So?" Mina said. Her face was twisted from the strain of the sounds. Boo had his hands over his ears.

"Hansi and Madrigal must have started up a huge great machine, underground," Leo said.

"Yes, but what *for*?"

"A generator, something electrical... Oh, lor!"

"Oh lor, *what*?"

"Look, Mina: it could be that they're starting up that army of theirs! Feeding them pow or whatever."

"You mean, they're activating the soldiers? But why? What against? There's only *us*, we don't deserve a whole robot army..."

"The thunder," Boo said. "It's for them, up there." He pointed to the sky.

"I'd forgotten the other noise," Leo admitted. "Maybe that's it. There must be something up there, coming at us, and Hansi and Madrigal need their army to fight it."

"No," Mina said. "It's more likely that Up There and Down Here are both parts of the same thing. I mean, Hansi and Madrigal mean to invade *some* time, and perhaps *this* is the time, because of us knowing about their invasion plan and their secret army and everything."

"Ma and Da," Boo said. "It's Ma and Da." He thrust his chin at the sky. "They're coming soon," he said. A tear ran down his cheek. He started running blindly, holding his hands up to the sky. Mina caught him.

"What do you mean, Ma and Da?" she said.

But Boo would only say, "I want my ma and I want my da and they're coming soon."

Mina and Leo stared at each other, over Boo's head, then shrugged. Mina said. "You take him – don't let him go! – and I'll find out what's happening to the Princess."

She began walking towards the great entrance of the Palace; but stopped when she felt the earth begin to shake under her feet.

The distant, thunderous rumble that shook the sky became suddenly a shattering bellow: and there it was – you could see it! – a blunt-nosed, shark-like ship, silver and black against the greenish sky! You could pick out its markings, wonder at the shifting, fire-flecked cushion of pure energy it rested on... until the weapon-fringed nose dipped, and the ship lurched at Argosy IV like a pike about to snatch its prey.

"Paxforce ship!" Leo shouted. "And it's coming in!"

"Mind me! Don't hit me!" Boo trumpeted, as the ship, pointing straight at him, seemed to swell and fill the sky. "It's come to *save* us, silly!" Mina shouted at him. She was jumping up and down and waving her arms. "Come on! Come on! We're here!"

Leo's excitement was already over. "Where are you, you pigs?" he muttered; and looked behind and around him for Hansi and Madrigal. He thought. They must have expected something like this, surely? Didn't the generator noise from the funnel prove that they were up to something? And haven't they got to get rid of me and Mina and Boo?

There they were! By the mouth of the funnel! Hansi with some sort of gun in his hand; Madrigal raving at him, telling him, "No! Don't shoot!" Leo could not hear the words, but that was what Madrigal must be saying, "Don't shoot the children. It's too late." And then she'd say, "Our army! Bring the soldiers out! Use them to destroy the Paxforce ship, kill its crew – then we can see to the children!"

Now the ship's bulk was low in the sky. It sprouted slender black mushrooms, its landing gear. It rested on columns of dragon fire and slid its dark bulk down them. Its sides began to gape black holes; human figures filled the holes. The figures carried things that glinted. Arms, weapons.

Now the ship was almost on the ground. A hot wave of gritty, pulsing air buffeted Leo's face. The air had that familiar electrical smell, that iodine smell. Then – nothing: the ship was down, the drives were cut. Already, Paxforce soldiers were jumping out of the hatches. From this distance, they looked no bigger than tabletop models. Mina hurrayed, Boo foghorned and pranced. Leo looked behind and around him...

And felt sick. Robot soldiers were pouring out from under the ground, spewing out so fast that the new-comers blundered into those already forming ranks. Hansi and Madrigal had to yell, "Make room! Open out!"

Leo swung Mina round to look. She said, "Oh no, please not! It can't happen, it mustn't!"

"It has," Leo said. "Hansi and Madrigal detected the Paxforce ship. They've mobilized their army."

Boo had noticed nothing. He pranced and cheered and waved his plump arms. Mina went to him. "No, leave him," Leo said. "He's happy. For a moment. Look at the robots. *Study* them."

He and Mina looked. The robot soldiers still poured out of the ground; still jostled and stumbled. Hansi ran back and forth, his balloon body bouncing on his bolster legs, shouting, "Over here! Yes, *here*! Spread out, make room!"

"Why's he *shouting* at them?" Mina said. "I'd have thought —"

"Me too. You'd think they'd be linked by some sort of command network... Hansi or Madrigal would just push buttons on a computer or speak into a mike or something."

"Look at Madrigal," Mina said. The woman was, again, in one of her furies. This time her fury was directed at an apparatus she held in her hand, connected to a box on a shoulder sling. "Ah!" Leo said. "So that's what's gone wrong! Communication gear no good!"

"It's all a mess, thank heaven!" Mina said. "Look at the robots! Falling over each other! What ought *we* to do?"

"Don't know. It's not *all* a mess. That lot over there – look at them!"

A group of robot soldiers, perhaps a hundred of them, had formed a column in ranks of three. Each soldier carried a weapon at an identical slope. Each began running, left-right, left-right, at the identical easy speed. They headed for the Paxforce ship.

Boo saw them. As Mina's had done, his face collapsed in dismay. "Go away!" he shouted. "Bad! Horrible! Pudding faces!"

"Pudding faces..." Leo murmured. True. The robot faces were featureless blanks, mouthless, noseless, hairless, eyeless. But also tireless, fearless, pitiless, ruthless.

"What do we *do*?" Mina repeated. She looked out over the mean landscape. The Paxforce troops were on their way. Some ran, others rode in on wide-tracked weapon carriers. Very soon, human would meet robot.

105

"I know!" Leo said. "You take care of Boo. I'm off!"

"Off where? We mustn't split up, you can't just —"

"I'm going to tell the soldiers – *our* soldiers – that the Doops' communications system has broken down."

"Yes, yes, tell them! But come straight back!"

"I'll be back."

He ran. Hansi must have seen him go and guessed his reason, for two robot soldiers lifted their weapons and fired. Their shots went wild. Hansi himself picked up his gun and aimed. A rock near Leo's feet exploded into orange and violet flame. Near him, a robot fired. The head of the soldier standing in front of him was blown off his shoulders. Mina, horrified, gasped. Boo shouted, "Can't shoot straight, *stupid*!"

Leo kept running. When his lungs were about to burst, an arm swept him upwards and on to a Paxforce weapon carrier and a man's voice said, "What's up, Doc?"

"Bugs Bunny," Leo gasped. "I've seen... those old... cartoons..."

Seconds later, he'd told the soldier all he needed to know. The soldier said, "Great. Fine. Understood," and pushed a Service helmet over Leo's head. "Listen, Bugs," he said to Leo. "Keep down low. There's going to be a fight. You stay out of the way."

"My sister! My brother!"

"Just keep down *low*."

The Storm Breaks

Hansi, his purple face spraying sweat, shouted, "Over there! That is the enemy! Fire at the enemy!" Behind him, Madrigal screeched, "*There*, morons! Fire at *them*!" and tried to push robot soldiers into position.

Often, the orders were obeyed. The ranks-of-three detachment seemed to know what it was doing: robot guns gave their yelping bark. Exploding bullets spat fire, pulverizing metal, rock and, sometimes, robot soldiers standing in the way.

The Paxforce troops moved forward steadily. In the carriers, Leo asked his soldier, "Why don't we fire back?"

"Your sister and brother, remember?" the soldier answered. "We might hit them. We can't open up until we know where they are."

"They're over there," Leo shouted, pointing.

"Got to know *exactly* where they are," the soldier said. The carrier rolled steadily on.

"Keep your head down!" Mina shouted at Boo. He would keep bobbing his head up to see the advancing Paxforce troops. They were closer than ever now. They looked calm, unhurried, unbeatable. But more robot soldiers were beginning to act sensibly. The same idea seemed to be entering many faceless heads: *there* was the enemy, you had to *fire* at the enemy. The air over Mina's head twitched with flying bullets.

"I've got to see!" Boo said, and before Mina could stop him, raised his head yet again. The rock sheltering them vanished in a ball of bellowing flame. Boo's hair was clouded in brown dust. "Careful, do be careful!" he told himself, sternly; and lay flat beside Mina with his head in his arms.

Now the Paxforce troops were so close that voices could sometimes be heard. "Mina!" the voices shouted. "Mina! Show yourself! Mina! Boo! Where are you?"

Mina understood: Paxforce could not open fire until she and Boo were located. "Stay down!" she hissed at Boo; and made herself stand upright, waving her arms. "OK, get down!" a Paxforce voice shouted. She flung herself on the ground, trembling. The rocks around belched fire and dust as robot bullets hit. Boo said, "You told *me* to stay down, then *you* got up!"

'I know, I know," Mina said. She was shaking too much to explain.

As she spoke, the solid ground heaved and juddered – the heavy air punched and pulsed – the world shook itself apart.

At last, Paxforce had opened fire.

The din was terrifying. Mina and Boo clutched at stony ground and pulpy vegetation with white-knuckled fingers. They screamed between clenched teeth, saw coloured flashes through the lids of their tightly closed eyes, tried to lock their shuddering brains shut against unbearable noise.

But their minds hardened. Boo said, "I'm sick of this!" and sat up, lower lip stuck out and eyes open. Mina, too, cautiously raised herself and looked about her.

She saw massacre.

The robot soldiers fired their weapons ceaselessly. The sky howled with flying bullets and the earth blazed with fiery explosions. "But they're not doing it *properly*," Boo said. "Not *aiming*."

The Paxforce had become a killing machine. The soldiers simply found cover, settled themselves comfortably, aimed, fired and kept firing. With each shot, a robot soldier exploded into a mess of shredded plastic, glittering metal, flying limbs.

A robot hand whirled through the air and stirred a small cloud of dust as it thumped down near Mina and Boo.

The hand was still attached to metal bones, coloured wires and an electronic function box. The joined fingers were still wrapped round the plastic stock of a weapon. The forefinger of the hand still pumped a non-existent trigger.

Mina thought, It's disgusting, horrible. I should *feel* something! She felt nothing but fascination.

It was the same with Boo. "Still working," he remarked, and imitated the pumping forefinger. Then he lost interest and looked at the battle.

It was safe to watch it. Mina and Boo were like spectators at a tennis match, close to but not part of the action. After a while, this life-and-death match seemed almost uninteresting. The winners kept winning, the losers kept losing. Robot soldiers, methodically slaughtered, were blown apart; and replaced by more robot soldiers from the seemingly endless reserves underground.

When Boo said, "Where's Leo?" the question was more interesting to Mina than the battle. She managed to pick him out. "There! Can you see, Boo? Leo's there, in that weapon carrier!" Its weapons went blat-blat-blat-blat, as regularly as a computer doing a print-out. Just as regularly, clusters of robot soldiers fell or burst apart.

"He's seen us!" Boo shouted. "He's waving!"

They waved back. But Leo kept waving – waving frantically – waving and pointing. "Trying to tell us something," Boo said, frowning.

At last they read Leo's message. Behind the piled bodies of robot soldiers, the heads of Hansi and Madrigal showed. Hansi's blob of a face seemed, even at this distance, creased into a mask of delight. Madrigal seemed to be dancing with joy.

"Why?" Mina began to say. Before she could finish, Hansi's voice answered her. He bent his head over a gadget in his hand, and spoke. His voice, vastly amplified, roared out, louder even than the noise of battle. "THREE TWO SEVEN!" bellowed the voice. Then, "WHAT, MADRIGAL? YOU THINK SO? OK. THREE TWO SEVEN, FOUR TWO EIGHT, NINE – WHAT? I AM ALREADY SAYING THAT – NINE THREE EIGHT! SO!"

Suddenly, horribly, the battle changed. Hansi's voice bellowed strings of numbers; and now, the robot

110

weapons were aimed with a purpose. Now, the soldiers efficiently took cover behind fallen bodies. Now, their bullets found Paxforce targets. A weapon carrier rocked and sprouted coloured fire. It survived but near it human voices shouted urgently.

"Hansi and Madrigal!" Mina said. "Oh, God! They've done it! They're in control!"

"FIVE FIVE THREE!" shouted Hansi's voice. "YES, FIVE FIVE THREE — THEN MORE THREE TWO SEVEN I THINK... NO, ZERO ZERO ZERO... FIVE FIVE THREE! FIVE FIVE THREE!"

Already Mina was beginning to break the code. Three Two Seven — that must mean spread out, make room for more soldiers to arrive. The other number groups must be aiming and firing codes. Zero Zero Zero meant cancel the last order. But Five Five Three...?

"FIVE FIVE THREE!" Hansi's voice shouted yet again. "OH YES, FIVE FIVE THREE!" His voice sounded almost as if it were telling a joke.

Slowly and smoothly, Five Five Three rose from the ground.

Five Five Three was no joke.

Perhaps it rose from the mouth of the tunnel. Perhaps it had crawled along the passages leading to the underground stronghold and emerged from some other place. Certainly it was terrifying, if only because of its massive simplicity.

A tower of gleaming metal. A flexible tower that bent and turned as if seeking something. A tower that rose and expanded, silkily telescoping itself to the height of a house — then sprouted, from its innumerable windows, articulated metallic arms holding weapons. The weapons swung to point in one direction: towards Paxforce.

Boo said, "No! No! It mustn't!"

"FOUR TWO EIGHT. NINE THREE EIGHT!" roared Hansi's voice.

"Stop that!" Boo cried. "I won't let you!" Furious-eyed, he started running towards Hansi and the evil tower. Mina did not see him go. She was thinking of the codes – and praying, Please let me be dreaming, please don't let that tower thing be real...

A bullet screamed past Boo. It was so close that he stopped to feel his head. It was still there. He pouted, said, "Got to stop them!" and began running again. He would have to go the long way, behind the robot soldiers, not in front of them. "You be *very careful*," he told himself. His legs pumped, his feet pounded. Bullets flew, lots of them. Some cracked like whips, some screamed. His chest hurt. He wanted to sit down and cry. He said, "Pig! Stop it!" and kept running. He was making for Hansi. Hansi was the pig who had to be stopped.

"SEVEN FOUR THREE!" the pig yelled.

Madrigal was shouting in Hansi's ear. "Moron!" she yelled. "Do I have to do *everything*? Get it *right*, get the tower *firing*! The code is Seven Three Four, not Seven Four Three! For heaven's *sake*!"

"ZERO ZERO ZERO," Hansi bellowed. He drew a deep breath. Now came the order that would finish this battle, any battle: "SEVEN, THREE —"

A cannonball hit him in the stomach. It hit him so hard that he dropped his microphone and fell backwards, bringing Madrigal down with him.

The cannonball, Hansi realized, must have been the

head of the little boy standing over him. The boy had grabbed the microphone. He was shouting into it. Amazingly, unbelievably, the little boy spoke in his – Hansi's – voice!

"ONE TWO THREE!" bawled the little boy. "FOUR FIVE SIX! ZERO ZERO ZERO! TWICE ONE IS TWO! THREE TWO ONE! TWICE FOUR EIGHT!"

Madrigal groaned. "My *arm*, you fat *lout*, it's *broken*!"

Hansi was winded, he could not get up. He reached out to the boy, "Good boy, give me that! Please! *Nice* boy!" The boy moved away from Hansi's outstretched hand and said, "FIVE SIX SEVEN, ZERO ZERO ZERO, HELLO MINA, HELLO LEO, THIS IS ME! TWICE FIVE TEN, THREE TWO ONE, ZERO ZERO ZERO."

All around the little boy, robot soldiers picked up weapons and put them down – turned left, right – faced the front, the rear – shot the earth, the sky or each other.

The great armoured tower waved its weapons at the sky. Occasionally a weapon fired. Nothing was hit.

There was a booming in the sky, then an orange glow fringed with black smoke, then an irregular series of small explosions; and finally a long, drawn-out fumbling, slithering, grinding sound.

The Clegg ship had landed on Argosy IV.

A girl of incredible beauty walked serenely onto the battlefield. She wore a crown, carried a sceptre. Her fur-trimmed velvet robes flew like angel's wings from her shoulders. Behind her were ranged her Warrior Queen and some twenty Doops.

She halted, drew herself up, lifted her lovely chin and

shouted, "This must stop! I rule here! This is my kingdom! Fighting is bad. Battles are worse. War is worst of all. Stop!"

Her words were met with almost complete silence. Then Boo's voice, hugely amplified, said, apologetically, "We *have* stopped. All over now."

The Princess said, "Oh." Then she turned to her Doops and said, "I want this place thoroughly cleaned up."

The main port of the Clegg's ship opened. Two figures appeared and descended. Three figures rose from the battlefield, silent now. All the figures ran towards each other and merged, clasped in each other's arms.

When her parents' arms went round her, Mina could only say, "Ma...! Oh, Ma...! Oh, Da!"

Leo could say nothing at all.

Boo said, "*Knew* they'd come. *Told* you so." Laboriously, he stood on his head.

Tumbling Crown

Saying these few things took time. When the time was up, the war was over. The Paxforce troops were already loading weapons and supplies on to the weapon carrier. Two stood guard over Hansi and Madrigal. Madrigal waved her arms and fingers and shouted at Hansi. Hansi called the soldiers "his dear friends", and smiled hopefully with his head on one side. The soldiers silently brushed past him.

The robot army was frozen, as if the soldiers had been playing Statues. They stood, sat or lay in grotesque attitudes. From time to time a trigger finger curled, by delayed action, on a trigger and a shot rang out. Occasionally there were whole volleys of these random shots. Then Hansi would smile more widely than ever and shrug his shoulders; and Madrigal would complain, "*Really*! Too ridiculous! I mean, really, Hansi, you could at *least* switch them *off*."

When Mina was able to talk properly, she said, "Oh, the Princess! Ma – Da – there she is, you must meet her, she's the only beautiful thing on Argosy IV!" She ran to the Princess and took her hand. The Princess said, "I am very busy. I will receive your parents later. In the Palace."

"But, please, Supa! They're longing to meet you!"

"You should call me Your Majesty, how many times must I tell you? You upset me with your thoughtlessness. And I mustn't be upset because I'm going to have a baby. A little baby..."

Again, Mina felt her throat tighten with pity for the lovely toy that knew so much and so little; again, as so often before, she felt furious impatience. She bit her lip, turned away and rejoined her parents. "She won't come, she's gone all queenly," she told them. "Worse than that – Queen *Motherly*! Ooops, here she comes after all. Don't forget to call her Your Majesty!"

They watched the upright little figure, glowing like a lighted Christmas tree, walk towards them. They heard a sudden flurry of shots from a distant heap of piled robot bodies. The Princess's Doops – even the Warrior Queen – turned their heads uneasily; the Princess walked on unheeding.

Now the Princess was very close. Gravely, she adjusted the crown on her head and the royal smile on her face —

There was a short, vicious, slapping sound, and a ball of fire; the Princess's crown was spinning high in the air, glittering and turning; and the Princess was suddenly a smoking heap of velvet and pearls, satin

116

and fur, bright jewels and blackened plastics.

Mina struggled frantically in her father's arms, fighting, screaming, beating at him. "Let me go to her!" she begged.

"It's no good, Mina. It's over. There's nothing you can do. Over, all over."

"Where's the hero?" the Paxforce Commander said. He sat in the command cabin of the Paxforce ship; a small, steely man with short, steely hair.

The Clegg family was ranged in front of the Commander. His desk was flanked by control-and-command buttons and displays. In the very centre of the desk lay a huge, brightly coloured medal hammered out of scrap aluminium.

"I'm the hero," Boo said. "I'm here."

"Step forward, hero, and receive your medal," said the Commander.

"What's it for?" Boo said, suspiciously.

"For being a good mimic and head-butter. And for conspicuous gallantry in the face of the enemy. Come here, boy."

Boo came forward. The Commander placed the medal round Boo's neck. The medal had a sash of scarlet.

Boo said, "What's conspic— conspicky—"

"Conspicuous gallantry. That means being brave. You *were* brave, weren't you?"

"Course I was."

"There you are, then. You've won a medal."

"It's a nice medal," Boo said, no longer suspicious. "Can I wear it all the time?"

"All the time."

"Well, thank you for my nice medal."

"Don't thank me. Thank Technical Sergeant Venn.

117

He made it," said the Commander. He pushed buttons. The door of his cabin opened and two big Marines entered. "SIR!" they said, in chorus.

"This is a hero. Take him to Sergeant Venn."

"SIR!"

Acting as one, they seized Boo's upper arms, lifted him up and carried him away. Boo beamed. The door closed.

"Right," said the Commander. "Down to business."

"The Doops," said the Commander. "What's to be done about them?"

"That's easy, isn't it?" Tom Clegg said. "Simply de-activate them. Switch them off. And that's that."

Nobody spoke till Leo said, "No, that's not fair. They've a right to live."

"*Live?*" said the Commander. "How can they live? They're not living beings. They're automata. They're just machines, aren't they?" He swung his head to Mina. "What do you say, young lady?"

"I think Leo's right," Mina said. "They're machines, but not *just* machines. I mean, foxes and mice aren't *just* animals, robins and seagulls aren't *just* birds..."

"You've lost me," said the Commander.

Leo said, "I know what she means. Look: there's roast duck for dinner, right? But then there's also the pet duck, the one with the funny name and everything. The family pet. And that duck's not the same as the other duck, the roast one."

"Go on," said the Commander, rubbing his forehead.

"Well, what Mina means and what I mean *is*, that the Doops aren't just machines, they're – they're..."

"They're special," Mina said. "Special to us, any-

118

how. So let them live. You know Madra, the Warrior Queen, the one with the plumes and the fantastic gear? You could put her in charge. She'll lead them, she knows what to do. Then the Doops can live out their natural lifespan. There's nothing to be afraid of, she's not really a warrior, she just dresses up. She's the one you need. I mean, someone's got to be their leader now the Princess is gone."

Suddenly, Mina burst loudly into tears. "Supa, poor Supa!" she cried. "It's so unfair! That bullet hitting her, just any old bullet, it wasn't even *aimed*... She was so lovely, she shouldn't have died *ever*!"

The Commander had always addressed Mina as Young Lady. Now he said, "My dear, listen to me. Listen carefully. You really mean what you say?"

Mina nodded violently through her sobs.

"Then, my dear, let's tell ourselves a story. Let's suppose that the Princess is alive. Suppose that her creators, Hansi and that woman..."

"Hansi and Madrigal."

"Of course. Suppose that Hansi and Madrigal make the Princess's dream come true. They construct a baby for her; a baby as lovely as you say the Princess was. Are you listening?"

"Yes."

"Then continue the story! Take this handkerchief, dry your eyes. Go on with the story."

"Well, she's *happy*!" Mina began. "She's happy with her baby! She dresses it, talks to it, puts it to bed and everything..."

"Go on, my dear."

"She does all the things mothers do. She watches it grow."

"*What*?" said the Commander, sharply.

119

"She watches it grow," Mina said. Then, "Oh . . .!"

Leo said, "The Commander's right, Mina. The Princess couldn't grow. The baby wouldn't grow or change either. The two of them would remain the same for ever, like a picture in a frame, never changing. And after a time, the Princess would get fed up. You know what she was like, Mina."

Mina shook her head and said, "She was lovely! She shouldn't have been killed like that! I wish she could have gone on for ever!"

The Commander said, "You don't mean that, my dear. Those foxes and mice, those birds you talked about – do they live for ever? Do *we*? Life, growth, change, death: that's the rule, Mina. It's a good rule."

There was a long silence. Then Mina said, "I'm all right now. I don't need your handkerchief any more. Do you want it back? It's a bit messy."

The Commander said, "It's a Paxforce-issue handkerchief. I'd better have it back."

She went to him and gave him the handkerchief. She whispered something in his ear. No one heard what she said. But they did hear the Commander say, "Thank *you*, my dear!"; and saw him briskly and efficiently kiss Mina's cheek.

"Right," said the Commander. "We've settled the Doop question, haven't we? They're to live out their natural span?"

"If they *can*," Ellie Clegg said.

"Meaning?"

"We don't know how much the Doops depend on humans – Hansi and Madrigal. Perhaps they supply the brainbox, the Doops just follow their program. Without Hansi and Madrigal, the Doops die."

The Commander pushed a button. The Marines appeared. "Bring in the two prisoners."

Madrigal came in like a clothes line in a high wind, flapping her uninjured arm wildly. Hansi smirked, writhed and called the Commander, "Dear Captain, Sir." The Commander cut them down like a sickle. "Simply tell us," he said, "if the Doops are self-supporting, whether they can go on working without you."

"With just the *littlest* adjustment, dear Captain, Sir," Hansi said. "Just the slightest re-programing..."

"Oh, shut *up*, Hansi, you're always so *ridiculous*... Of *course* they can, don't be absurd, you don't think we'd have put them on the *market* if they weren't *absolutely* self-sufficient?"

"Pow," Leo interrupted. "They have to have pow, don't they? On Earth, they were sort of charged off the mains. But here, they have to get pow."

"Oh, *that*!" Madrigal said, waving her bracelets. "Madra, the one you call the Warrior *Queen*, sees to all *that*, you've seen her *doing* it. Now I really must *go*. I have things to *attend* to. So if you don't *mind* —"

"I do mind," the Commander said. "You're not going anywhere. You will appear before the relevant Earthside courts to answer a number of charges. A great number. Even those nets your Doops used to trap the children are illegal. Then there's the matter of your private army, your alleged attempt at a galactic invasion, armed resistance to Paxforce, et cetera. The courts will attend to all that. None of my business, thank heaven. But it is my business to hold you as prisoners until further orders from Earthside."

Madrigal screeched and flailed. Hansi deflated, slowly, and seemed to sink into himself. But he found enough air in him to say, "But dear Captain, Sir, what you call our private army was a technical exercise, nothing more! And a most useful exercise, surely you agree? So useful to someone like *you*, dear Captain – a gallant warrior, a fighting man! Let us suppose, say, that Earth is threatened by some wicked power... that more soldiers are urgently needed... Would you not welcome the splendid soldiers we created?"

"You're very considerate," the Commander said, icily. Then, "Tell me something: these robot soldiers of yours; why shape them like human beings? Why give them arms and legs and hands and all the rest of it?"

Madrigal shouted, "I'd have thought that perfectly *obvious*! I mean to say, who wants obscene little *boxes* covered with *buttons*? I mean, they might *win* a war – so might an enormous *bomb* – but what's the good of that? What happens *next*? Where's your *victory*?"

"Go on," said the Commander.

"Well, I mean, suppose we conquer Earth and we walk in as *invaders*. Well, how pointless can you *get*? We've blasted the enemy, laid the place utterly waste. What good's that? I mean, dear man, we want to use the enemy's *resources*, don't we? I mean, your soldiers hold guns in their *hands*, they pull *triggers* with their *fingers*; they drive *vehicles*, handle *equipment*. So *our* soldiers need hands and fingers – and arms and legs for that matter – so that they can *truly* conquer..."

She stopped, gasped and covered her mouth with a long-nailed hand. Hansi gave a whimpering groan. "Not that I'm admitting for a *moment*," she began.

"Not that you're admitting for a moment," the Commander said in a voice like sandpaper. To the Marines, he said, "Take them out. Lock them up."

"SIR!" said the Marines.

Goose, Swan and Duckling

Next day, Leo and his father walked round the battle-field. "Da, how much longer do you think we'll be here?"

"I don't know. Until Earthside sends a ship, I suppose, to collect us, and Hansi and Madrigal and so on and so on. Days, a week. I just don't know."

"Why can't we just blast off in our own ship? I want to go home."

"Well, there are certain difficulties with our ship. Nothing major, you understand. Just little difficulties. Soon have it fixed."

Leo did not answer. There was no need to. He knew all about Little Difficulties, Nothing Major. He sighed and look at the battlefield.

Weapon carriers were now being used as earthmovers, or rather, bodymovers. They scooped up robot soldiers and stacked them in rectangular heaps. Leave the place as you'd hope to find it, Leo thought. The bodies looked awful, even though they were not "real" and human. Dead limbs and blank faces glistened nastily, wetted by a thin drizzle from the grey-green sky.

"I don't know how you stuck it, Leo," Tom Clegg said. "I'm sick of the place already. It's a horrible little world. And there you were, locked up in that hutch of yours."

"Oh, it was all right. I suppose," Leo said. "The Doops can't tie knots. I escaped whenever I felt like it. Not that there was anywhere to go." He became silent, remembering. Then he said, "And I did become a royal prince in a plumed hat! A married man! Almost a father! At least, that was what the Princess had in mind."

"Poor Princess," said his father. "And poor Mina. She's still not over it."

Leo changed the subject. "Look at the tower!" he said. "Still looks a bit frightening, doesn't it? The soldiers are blowing it up in an hour or so. What a waste."

"This whole place is a waste," Tom Clegg said. "A desert. Arid. Useless."

"But the mountain's quite interesting," Leo said. "Weird, anyway. It's got power in it, or something."

Tom Clegg stopped walking to stare at the mountain. Leo saw a certain look come into his father's face, a look he had often seen before: a speculator's look, the "Just possibly" look. "Da!" he said. "You're not getting one of your ideas, are you?"

"Do you know, Leo," his father said, "an idea has just struck me. It's just possible that..."

"Da! It's just a grotty little old mountain! Leave it alone!"

His father did not hear him. He was flapping at himself, feeling this pocket and that, checking for this instrument and the other.

"Da, we'll be eating soon, hadn't we better get back?"

But his father was already walking away from him fast, heading for the mountain.

Leo sat on a rock and watched him go. There was no point in following him. "He's off again," Leo muttered. "Off on a wild-goose chase after a swan that turns out to be an ugly duckling."

This brilliant phrase cheered him up a little. He would use it to explain Da's absence to the rest of the family.

Nobody seemed to notice the brilliant phrase. Leo was furious.

"It was very clever, I *did* laugh," Mina said. They were waiting to see the tower blown up.

"You never laugh at my jokes," Leo said. "Yet when you're with your feeble friends, your girl chums, it's all giggle, giggle, giggle, ha, ha, ha."

"Liar," Mina said.

Boo said, "He's not lying, it's all true, you go 'tee-hee-hee' and 'Ooooo!'" He gave an imitation of a giggle of girls. It was perfect.

"Very funny," Mina said sourly. "Of course, it's all completely different when you and your friends get together, isn't it? Hur-hur-*hur*, hur-hur-*hur*. Stupidest noise I've ever — Hey, look! They're starting!"

The tower went up with less of a bang than expected. It was a disappointment. "Is that all?" Boo said.

"They've used that wrap-round explosive like sticky tape," Leo explained. "It just slices things in two instead of blowing them to bits. Give me the good old days when bangs were bangs."

Boo went "B–b–BANG... WRUMPH!", practising explosions. His imitations were better and much louder than the real thing. Mina said, "Boo, don't, you go right through my head!" Boo did more explosions. Mina suddenly lost her temper and slapped his arm, not hard; but hard enough to cause his eyes to fill with tears. "Hitting people!" he said, and trotted away. "Boo, come back! I'm sorry!" But he ran on without a backward look.

Now Mina looked tearful. In the old days, she was never tearful. Leo said, "Oh, come *on*, Mina, it's all right," and awkwardly put an arm round her shoulders. But this only made her cry in earnest.

Boo walked towards the remains of the tower; Mina walked in the opposite direction; Leo was left standing. He decided to follow Mina. He caught up with her and said, "Look, Mina, if there's something – if there's anything..."

She said, "Oh, it's me being stupid, it's nothing to do with you or anyone else."

"It's got to be something or someone. I mean, this isn't like you."

"It's the Princess. I can't get over it."

"But you *must* get over it. It isn't as if she was a real person – a real animal, even, a dog or cat. I mean, it's ridiculous to go on mooning and mourning over a machine."

Mina said, "Have you got your watch?"

"Yes, of course," he showed her the standard-issue watch/radio on his wrist.

"Not that one," she said. "That's just *a* watch. I meant *your* watch. The antique one."

"You know I've got it. I always wear it."

"And your mascot thing, that crystal doll, you always carry that too, don't you? And you'd hate to lose it?"

"Well, yes."

"There you are, then. Your watch, your lucky charm – multiply them by a million or two and you'll understand how I feel about the Princess. It's hard to explain... She was a sort of *pattern* for something. Something better than us..."

"And worse."

"Yes, worse too. All the same..."

"I know what you mean. I do, really. But try to get over it. You matter more than ever she did. To me, anyhow."

"That's not bad, coming from a brother!" she said. All at once, she looked herself again.

"Let's go and find Boo," she said. "I don't like the idea of him getting too close to the tower."

Boo wasn't at the tower. "We shooshed him away," a soldier told Mina. "Didn't want him playing around in all this mess. I think he went that way." He pointed to the Commander's quarters.

"He'll be fooling around with the Paxforce ship's crew," Leo said. "As usual."

They went to the Commander's cabin first. It was the polite thing to get his permission. The Marine guarding the door of the Commander's cabin was by now an old friend. Without moving from "attention", he squinted horribly at Leo and made a menacing "Grrr!" sound at Mina. She pressed one of the gleaming buttons on his chest and made a noise like an electric buzzer. "Can we go in" she said.

"I'll see, Miss."

Then, "SIR!" and the Commander's voice, and his smile.

"We want to find Boo," Mina said. "I was nasty to him and he ran off. And now I'm a bit anxious."

The Commander pressed buttons. Screens showed various parts of the ship. At last, Boo was located.

He was in the Armoury, a top-security section in which no one was allowed. A massive Marine in a spotless T-shirt was loading Boo into the cage of a little lift. The lift was designed to carry missiles to the ship's weapons. Now it carried Boo. He was wearing his medal. The Marine pressed a button and Boo disappeared upwards.

The Commander said, "Good God!" and pressed another button. Boo reappeared on another screen. He had reached a higher level. A second Marine, with ginger hair, was lifting Boo out of the lift's cage and placing him at the top of a shute. The shute's function was to dispose of spent missile cases. Now it carried Boo. Clutching his medal in both hands, he slid down the shute. The first Marine collected him, placed him in the lift, and the game started all over again.

"Good God!" the Commander repeated. "I'll have to court-martial everyone!"

"Even Boo?" Leo said.

"Especially Boo. Tea or coffee?"

"Tea, please," Mina said. "I've lost my taste for coffee, ever since I smelled it coming out of the vent.

Where Hansi and Madrigal lived."

"*Hansi*!" the Commander said, disgustedly. "*Madrigal...*" He made a growling noise not unlike the Marine's.

Tom Clegg came back from the mountain, gathered his family around him and said, "We're rich!"

The family groaned as one. Boo said, "Story!" Leo said, "Not again?" Mina said. "Rich like last time, when they had to send out a rescue ship for us?"

Ellie put on an interested, wifely expression and said, "How exciting: tell us all about it!"

"Oh, you won't believe *me*," Tom said, in a martyred tone. "And you won't believe *these*." He reached into his pocket for a handful of coppery nuggets. He threw them on the table. They looked very small and uninteresting. "But you might believe Technical Officer Patel. He'll be with us in a moment, he's bringing some precision instruments and pieces from his lab. I just used what I was carrying. A simple voltmeter. Mind you, it's a very good little instrument..."

"What are you trying to tell us?" Ellie said, firmly but kindly.

"I thought I'd explained. We're rich. These little bits of rock from the mountain – I hacked them out with my hammer, I thought, 'Hello, there's something odd about you, something that rings a bell!' Well, I hacked them out and chopped them up and blow me down if... Oh, there you are, Patel. *You* tell them, they won't believe a word I say."

T/O Ved Patel blew in like a young, friendly gale. He seized hands and shook them – swept things on the table to one side – replaced them with small, costly scientific instruments. The instruments glittered. So did

T/O Patel. His hair was black, his eyes a brilliant brown and his white teeth flashed. He made Mina blink. "You're rich!" he said. "Did you know?"

"I did try to tell them," Tom said. "They weren't impressed."

"Oh, but you will be! Very soon! Immediately! Just watch, Mrs Clegg! Watch, all of you! Look: here is a sample of rock from the mountain. I take this piece – any piece will do —"

"Nothing up my sleeve," Leo whispered to Mina. "Positively no deception."

"Sh!" Mina said. She was following T/O Patel's every move with wide, admiring eyes.

"I place the little sample – so – on the voltmeter. There! What do you see?"

"Bit of rock on a thing," Boo foghorned, scornfully.

Mina said, "Shut up, Boo." She peered at the volt-meter and said, "Oh, look! There's a reading. One point four volts."

"Let me look," Leo said. He looked closely at the needle. "One point three seven, actually," he said, and whistled. Then, "Hey, that's not bad, Da! So we were right, weren't we? The Doops get their pow in the form of an electrical charge from the mountain. I always thought so. The mountain's an energy pile. That's really interesting!"

"No it's not," his father said. "Electricity crops up all over the place. Anywhere, everywhere. Electric eels, human bodies, this planet, Earth – everything runs on electricity. Or with it. Ved, show them the really interesting thing!"

"Right," said T/O Patel. "Mrs Clegg – take another piece of rock. A smaller piece. Yes, that little bit will do nicely. Place it on the meter... Yes, perfect. What reading do you see?"

Ellie said, "Point six three one."

"About half the voltage of the first sample." Tom said. "There you are, then. We're rich!"

"Rich is what you are, Tom!" said T/O Patel, beaming.

"Say it all again, very slowly," Ellie said. "I'm not with you."

"But it's obvious!" her husband shouted. "The voltage given is exactly proportional to the size of the sample! If a big piece gives two volts, a piece exactly half the size – half the bulk and weight – will give one volt. I mean, we can *show* you. Show them, Ved! There's an exact relationship between the mass of a sample and the voltage it delivers!"

"Voltage for how long?" Leo said.

"What's that? For how long? Oh, didn't I tell you? I'd have thought that was obvious too. I mean, Ved and I wouldn't be getting all worked up if the output was just *temporary* – if it just fizzled out. But it doesn't! It goes on and on! We've tried to drain various samples – to exhaust them, draw off all their energy – and of course, we *can* exhaust them, artificially. Ved will show you. Not that it matters. What does matter is, that left to themselves, the little darlings just keep dishing out volts!"

"You mean, they go on for ever?" Leo said. His face was pale with excitement. So was his mother's.

"No, not for *ever*, that's absurd, that would mean we'd discovered perpetual motion. There's no such thing as a free meal."

"But there is such a thing," Ellie said, "as a new power source for all kinds of micro-mechanisms and what-have-yous?" She was holding a chip of the mountain rock and gazing at it in a dazed, worshipful way.

Ved Patel said, "Look, Mrs Clegg, you know better than most people about Earth technology. You know all about the tools used for anything from an interplanetary voyage to timing a boiled egg. And micromechanisms... just think how many *you* use. Knowing all this, you know there are infinite uses for little bits of rock containing little voltages. *Infinite*."

"So, for us, there *is* such a thing as a free meal," Ellie said. Solemnly, she rose to her feet and kissed her husband.

"Free meal," Boo said. "I'm hungry."

An Earthside ship came, a ship so big that it could have found room for every trace of human existence on Argosy IV.

The ship scooped up Hansi and Madrigal and packed them away in locked and guarded cells.

It scooped up various kinds of Doops for Earthside analysis and study; various interesting bits and pieces from the underground stronghold; and Jeeves, who bowed slightly from the waist when the men came for him – and from then on pampered everyone aboard with cold drinks, hot snacks or whatever was required.

It scooped up the Clegg family, complete.

It could not take the Commander, for he had his own ship to look after and would go his own separate way. When the time came to say goodbye to him and his crew, Boo clamped himself round the leg of one of his favourite Marines and boohooed like a hundred foghorns all sounding at once. He had to be bribed to let go with a bugle, a Marine's dress hat and a sworn promise to meet again, Earthside.

Leo said nothing and did nothing while the goodbyes went on. He just stood like a statue. Yet nobody forgot to shake his hand and wish him well.

Mina said farewell to the Commander by flinging her arms round his neck and kissing him, in full view of crew members, soldiers and Marines. The Commander went very red.

When the time came for Mina to say farewell to T/O Ved Patel, she did not look at him. She merely extended a limp hand for him to shake. "That's because she's *shy*," Boo trumpeted. "She's *shy* because she thinks he's *handsome*. 'He's so handsome,' that's what you said, isn't it, Mina? *Isn't it?*"

Mina went even redder than the Commander.

Billionaire

The ship was grand as well as big. It was a GalaxTours cruiseliner specially commissioned for this one-off trip by various Earthside authorities and business interests. The Cleggs had never known such luxury. Each member of the family had its own cabin, use of the jacuzzi, games facilities, restaurants, video rooms and steward service.

Leo explored all these delights but his greatest pleasure was the flattering attention of the adult passengers. They all seemed to be important, mature, rich men and women. "Oh! You're Leo Clegg!" they'd exclaim, shaking him warmly by the hand. Then they offered him drinks, the use of their 3D viddy cameras, anything at all.

At first, Leo thought these people must be journalists drawn to him by his fascinating adventures on Argosy IV. Obviously they wanted his story. He gave it to them at full length, piling on the agony when he described his days in the hutch and his experiences as whipping boy.

Soon, though, he realized that he was not being listened to. People even interrupted him. "Your father," they would say. "Is there any chance of an introduction?"

"But," Leo replied, "he wasn't even *on* Argosy IV when I was being whipped! Or when I became a prince! And he never even knew the Princess!"

"No, of course, I realize that," would be the reply. "You and your sister – you had the real adventures. Fascinating. All the same, if you could possibly introduce me to your father..."

It puzzled him. Then Mina said, "Oh, you are dim! They're not interested in you or me, it's Da they're after! Because he's stinking rich!"

"But he can't be, he's Da. Poverty-stricken Da. And, anyway, we're only half-way to Earthside. Nothing can have happened yet!"

Ellie overheard this conversation. "You're living in the twenty-first century," she told Leo. "Things happen *fast*. News gets around almost before it's happened. Your father is already known as the Man with the Big Future, the next tycoon. Soon you'll have to call Da 'Father' or even 'Sir'. In public, anyhow." She laughed.

Leo looked thoughtful. "First I was a whipping boy, then a prince married to a fairy princess," he mused. "And now I'm son and heir to a billionaire!"

It sounded good. So good that Leo repeated the phrase. He even set it to music. "*Son* and *heir* to a

136

bill-ion-*aire*!" he sang, quietly.

The big ship drove on through space, every thrust of each drive unit taking it nearer home.

VAMPIRE MASTER
Virginia Ironside

There's something very sinister about Burlap Hall's new biology master, Mr A. Culard. He hates light, loves bats and eats dead flies! Now the other teachers are starting to behave oddly too. The question is: will young Tom and his friends, Miles and Susan, manage to get their teeth into the problem before it gets its teeth into them?

"A very funny novel which keeps up a steady pace of entertainment and suspense."
The Bookseller

"Entertaining... Hilarious moments."
The Junior Bookshelf

SPACEBOY AT BURLAP HALL
Virginia Ironside

As usual, Burlap Hall school is in a state of crisis. Headmaster Mr Fox is being threatened with closure by his longtime enemy Clive Nutter, now a Schools' Inspector. But that's nothing to the problems he's about to face. For one stormy night Orcon arrives out of nowhere with a green face, a fiendish giggle and all sorts of unearthly tricks up his glove. Once again it's up to Tom and his friends Miles and Susan to try and save the school from total disaster!

THE WORM CHARMERS
Nicholas Fisk

Shanta, Jen, Crump and Horrie are the WCs, the Worm Charmers. But, in this action-packed adventure, it's worms of a much nastier and more lethal nature that they're up against: human worms – with kidnapping and drug-trafficking on their minds. Fortunately, the WCs have a pendulum and a perceptive detective named Pollitt to assist them. But will this be enough to save the day?

"A rattling good story, complete with all the right ingredients. It is fast, funny and totally without pretensions." *The Sunday Times*

ANTAR AND THE EAGLES

William Mayne

"A head with a yellow eye and curved beak looked down at him from above. The beak took hold of him by the new waistcoat, gripped and shook him...

Antar knew he was being carried away toward the mountains by an eagle."

So begins Antar's extraordinary adventure. For it is not as food that the great bird takes him, but for a mission vital to the survival of the entire eagle race. Before he can begin his task, however, Antar must first learn how to be an eagle...

"A dazzling book and a classic addition to fairy-tale." *Naomi Lewis, The Observer*

"The most original writer for children in the land... Mayne at his inimitable best."
Brian Alderson, The Times

FREDDIE AND THE ENORMOUSE
Hugh Scott

After the death of his parents, Freddie Faucet goes to live with his aunt, uncle and boisterous cousin Lindsay in their huge, luxurious old mansion. At first it seems like Paradise to Freddie. But then, one day, he sees something that makes his hair stand on end and his eyes go wide as saucers!

"A fast-moving, Tom-Sawyer-like adventure, very funny and in no way suitable for parents."
The Junior Bookshelf

"Hugh Scott knows exactly what he's about: the provision of thrills and spills."
The Times Educational Supplement

MORE WALKER PAPERBACKS

For You to Enjoy